Prais

"Shiloh's latest gracefully written contemporary romance thoughtfully explores the importance of faith and family during the holiday season."

—*Booklist* on *You Make It Feel like Christmas*

"Piper's internal battles between familial duty and a desire for independence are sensitively rendered, and readers will cheer her on as she tackles the racial stereotypes baked into the overwhelmingly white world of horse racing. Shiloh's fans will speed through this sweet, satisfying romance."

—*Publishers Weekly* on *A Run at Love*

"Shiloh radiates wisdom and sincerity. . . . *A Run at Love* is an inspiring friends-to-lovers modern romance about breaking barriers of ethnicity and gender and the importance of representation in nondiverse spaces. She brilliantly captures the drama of the equestrian world and the road to the Kentucky Derby while illuminating the emotional and experiential complexities of transracial adoption and identity."

—*Booklist* starred review of *A Run at Love*

"With faith and pop culture references from page one, Shiloh excels at growing multidimensional characters into friends, with a little help from family and God."

—*Library Journal* starred review of *The Love Script*

"Shiloh offers a sweet romance with a strong dose of spiritual truth."

—Pepper Basham, award-winning author of *Authentically, Izzy*, on *The Love Script*

"Toni Shiloh delivers another soulful, uplifting romance. . . . A swoon-worthy romance readers will adore."

—Belle Calhoune, bestselling author of *An Alaskan Christmas Promise*, on *The Love Script*

"I love a romance populated with characters you can truly root for. And this one has that and more. Coupled with Toni Shiloh's winning voice, it's a story not to be missed."

—Oprah Daily on *In Search of a Prince*

"This romance with a touch of mystery will stay with you long after The End."

—Rachel Hauck, *New York Times* bestselling author, on *In Search of a Prince*

"Toni Shiloh brilliantly weaves a romantic tale."

—Vanessa Riley, bestselling author of *Island Queen*, on *In Search of a Prince*

"Shiloh has penned yet another adorable and charming royal romance!"

—Melissa Ferguson, bestselling author of *Meet Me in the Margins*, on *To Win a Prince*

"Another winner that readers will enjoy from start to finish."

—Vanessa Miller, author of *Something Good*, on *To Win a Prince*

"Readers are going to be delighted by this endearing and adorable romance."

—Sarah Monzon, author of the Sewing in SoCal series on *The Love Script*

THE
Christmas
CATCH

Books by Toni Shiloh

From Bethany House Publishers

In Search of a Prince

To Win a Prince

Love in the Spotlight

The Love Script

A Run at Love

Novellas

You Make It Feel like Christmas

The Christmas Catch

THE *Christmas* CATCH

A SWEET HOLIDAY NOVELLA

TONI SHILOH

BETHANYHOUSE

a division of Baker Publishing Group
Minneapolis, Minnesota

Published by Bethany House Publishers
Minneapolis, Minnesota
BethanyHouse.com

Bethany House Publishers is a division of
Baker Publishing Group, Grand Rapids, Michigan

Printed in the United States of America

Library of Congress Cataloging-in-Publication Data
Names: Shiloh, Toni, author.
Title: The Christmas catch : a sweet holiday novella / Toni Shiloh.
Description: Minneapolis, Minnesota : Bethany House Publishers, a division of
    Baker Publishing Group, 2024.
Identifiers: LCCN 2024016023 | ISBN 9780764244698 (paperback) | ISBN
    9780764244728 (casebound) | ISBN 9781493449804 (ebook)
Subjects: LCGFT: Romance fiction. | Novellas.
Classification: LCC PS3619.H548 C57 2024 | DDC 813/.6—dc23/eng/20240415
LC record available at https://lccn.loc.gov/2024016023

Previously published in 2017 under the title *A Sidelined Christmas*.

Scripture taken from the New King James Version®. Copyright © 1982 by Thomas
Nelson. Used by permission. All rights reserved.

This is a work of fiction. Names, characters, incidents, and dialogues are products
of the author's imagination and are not to be construed as real. Any resemblance
to actual events or persons, living or dead, is entirely coincidental.

Cover illustration and design by Sarah Kvam

Author is represented by the literary agency of Rachel McMillan.

Baker Publishing Group publications use paper produced from sustainable forestry
practices and postconsumer waste whenever possible.

24 25 26 27 28 29 30   7 6 5 4 3 2 1

To the Author and Finisher
of my faith.

PROLOGUE

Wide receiver Jahleel Walker wiggled his fingers as he took his place on the line of scrimmage, waiting for the ball snap. The crowd roared for the San Antonio Desperados despite the fact that they were the away team. No way he wanted to lose to the Atlanta Falcons on Thanksgiving Day. Not if he could help it. He'd eat that turkey leg and make sure the holiday season was an epic one for the team.

Quarterback Colton Montgomery had called a pass route in the huddle, so Jahleel mentally ran the play while waiting for it to start. Since he'd started his career in the NFL eight years ago, the team had yet to earn the coveted Vince Lombardi trophy. If the Desperados could pull a win for the Super Bowl, maybe his father would finally approve of his career choice.

Get your head back in the game.

The ball snapped, and Jahleel took off. He juked a defensive player, arms pumping as he got to his spot and in the clear. His heart raced as he spun to catch the ball, watching as it spiraled through the air. *Come on, baby, come on.* When it neared, he pushed off on his toes, leaping into the air, arms splayed out to grab the ball. His hands gripped the pigskin, and he grinned, bringing it to his chest in one fluid motion as his body descended.

Someone slammed into his leg.

"Ahhhh!"

Excruciating pain exploded in his right knee as he collapsed onto the field, ball still clutched in his hands. He reached for his leg, gritting his teeth against the throbbing that radiated from his knee. The sound of a whistle barely penetrated the haze of agony. The white-hot heat caused his stomach to roll. He hissed, trying to keep his stomach contents inside.

A hand touched his shoulder. Someone removed his helmet. Another took the ball.

"Talk to me, Walker," Coach Brennan said.

"Right knee," Jahleel managed to grit out.

Hands stilled him as an athletic trainer examined his leg. A bout of pressure brought tears to his eyes, and a groan tore from his lips.

"What's wrong with it?" Coach asked.

Jahleel listened for the response, but silence greeted his ears. The trainer had either ignored Coach or simply shrugged in reply. Jahleel tried to lift his head to take a look, but a hand stayed him.

"You're going to feel more pressure."

Was that the team doc?

He inhaled, preparing himself, but it was no use. The agony shot up as the doc squeezed Jahleel's knee, shredding that ridiculous emoji scale for pain. Stars danced behind his eyelids, and he willingly succumbed to the darkness.

Chapter
ONE

God love her daughter, but going to early morning flag football games utterly exhausted Bebe. The two cups of coffee she'd drunk this morning hadn't adequately prepared her for ear-piercing whistles and yells from over-zealous parents. A couple of times she'd been tempted to snap at the cheering adults or offer them a sip of her coffee in hopes the liquid gold would calm them down. She wanted to enjoy watching her daughter play. Instead, the steady pounding in the back of her head had picked up its pace with every shout of approval.

As much as Bebe loved football—and she did with all her Falcons-lovin' heart—she valued sleep above all. Well, except the Lord.

She watched as Hope played defense, grabbing a flag to stop the other team from scoring. Bebe clapped her hands, happy to see her seven-year-old enjoying herself. As much as she complained about the cold and early hours, Bebe would be here next week just to see that same big smile on her daughter's face.

Finally the game ended, and Bebe got her sweaty but precious child into the car so they could go home and relax for the rest of the day. Soon she pulled her car into their driveway. With a turn of the key, the car shut off, bringing a moment of blissful silence.

"I can't believe we won, Mama," Hope said, unbuckling herself from her booster seat. She was skinny for a seven-year-old and didn't yet weigh enough to go without the safety precaution.

"You did good, baby." Bebe turned around, giving her daughter a quick kiss on the cheek. "Now, let's go in and get you cleaned up."

"Who's that, Mama?"

Bebe turned left, following the direction of her daughter's pointed finger. Thank goodness she had a good tint on her car windows. She wouldn't have to worry about someone seeing Hope point. Why did kids have to be so obvious in their curiosity?

The thought evaporated as soon as she saw the object of Hope's question.

Jahleel Walker. What on earth is he doing here?

Bebe's mind immediately transported her back in time to an era when she and Jay had laughed and joked, sitting on the front stoop while eating whoopie pies as children. Then her thoughts fast-forwarded to senior year, when their relationship took a dreamy turn. One filled with moonlight kisses under the oak trees.

Her heart pinched with concern, pulling her from memory lane. Jay wore a full-leg brace, and his parents flanked each side of him. He was hurt? Had it happened playing football or in some kind of car accident?

Bebe pushed the car door open, barely noting the sound of Hope's opening as well. Before she could caution her feet or brace her heart, she'd met the Walkers on their front lawn. "What happened?"

Mrs. Walker turned, her brow wrinkled with heartbreak. Bebe could only imagine the torture the woman was going through. No one wanted to see their child hurt, even if he stood at five-ten with corded muscle. A mother's heart would always see the baby she gave birth to.

"He tore three ligaments in his knee during the Thanksgiving game."

"What?!"

"That sucks," her daughter commented.

"Hope Marie Gordon!"

Her daughter stepped back, head dipping in shame. "Sorry, Mama."

Bebe shook her head, observing Jahleel. He turned slightly, eyes unfocused as he glanced her way. Her heart dipped again, but for a different reason this time. *Lord, have mercy! Why is he still so good-looking?* His warm brown skin leaned a little toward the lighter side but remained darker than her complexion. His coffee-colored eyes beckoned to her, daring her to remember their past.

She blinked, trying to bring herself back to reality. There should be a rule that you could only return to your hometown with a bald head and a potbelly. Yet the muscles rippling his forearms as he gripped the crutches could not be ignored, nor the way his full lips caught her attention. Jahleel Walker had only improved with time.

So not fair, Lord.

"We told him to come home. He needs someone to nurse him back to health." Mrs. Walker's hands fluttered nervously at her side.

Rumor had it that Jay had been kicked out of the Walker household shortly after his college graduation. Bebe had been shocked when she heard about it. Sure, everyone knew Reverend Walker didn't approve of his son's love of football, but surely that wasn't the reason his son had been banished from their home. Jay had confided in her about his dad's behavior when they were in high school, but once he'd cut off all ties with her, she lost the inside scoop.

Had Jay willingly returned home, or had there been no other choice? Then again, if he remained as heavily medicated as he was right now, his location might not even register. She gave an inward shake of the head.

"We need to get him inside," Reverend Walker stated.

Before Bebe could nod in agreement, Jahleel's eyes seemed to find their focus, narrowing on her face. Lines appeared around his eyes as they crinkled with amusement. "Bebe Willabee."

The use of her maiden name brought her eyes back to his mouth, perfectly framed by his neatly edged beard and mustache. *The better to catch your eye.*

A goofy smile appeared on his face. "Don't you look like a fine Georgia peach."

Wow. Those must be some Grade A painkillers. "Hey, Jay."

"Bebe." A chuckle slipped through, as if he found their reunion funny. She guessed the medication prevented him from feeling the awkwardness of a twelve-year reunion.

Her mouth twitched. Despite how their relationship ended, Bebe didn't know whether to laugh or cry at his current state.

Jahleel squinted as he looked back and forth between her and Hope. "Either you have a mini-me, or I'm more tired than I thought."

"He's funny, Mama." Hope giggled.

Jay tilted his head. "You have a child?"

"I do." Why did her stomach tense at the admission? It wasn't like she'd cheated on Jay. He'd broken up with her, and she found someone new. Though she could now say her ex-husband hadn't been the wisest choice.

"Huh? How did that happen?"

Reverend Walker shook his gray head. Lines drew his face

downward, either with age or disapproval. One could never tell with the good pastor. "You can catch up later, son. Let's get you inside."

"Bye, Bebe. I have to go before I get in trouble." Jay snickered with amusement.

She watched as Mrs. Walker held the door open while Reverend Walker escorted the prodigal into their brown craftsman bungalow.

A tug on her arm captured her attention. "Mama, I'm *hungry*."

"Sorry, pumpkin. Let's go get you a snack."

"Don't forget, I get a bath too!" For some reason, Hope loved baths in the middle of the day. She wasn't satisfied until rainbow-colored bubbles filled the tub.

Bebe led her daughter across the yard toward their home. It was practically identical to the Walkers' except the exterior had been painted slate gray. She glanced back, giving the Walker residence one more look.

Jahleel Walker.

Funny how a day could turn out completely different than it had started. Would he be okay? *Why do you care? You haven't talked to him in twelve years. Your best friend ghosted you to chase a football.*

Yet she couldn't help but identify with returning home feeling broken. After all, she'd been back in the coastal town of Peachwood Bay for three years now, still feeling a little lost. Bebe sighed and walked inside her childhood home—the one she rented from her folks.

Being back home had helped lessen the shock of her divorce. Too bad it hadn't removed the lingering disappointment or the stench of failure. It didn't help that Hope still wished for some type of relationship with her father—simply showing up for her birthday party would thrill her. Instead, Will's idea of a good relationship with his child was to let money do the talking. Bebe prayed Hope's disappointment would ease as she got ready to celebrate another birthday and Christmas without her father. Even though Will was slated to take Hope for the holiday, Bebe knew the other shoe would drop. It always did with him.

At least the Walkers were finally all together for the holiday season. A first in almost eight years. The speed with which Jahleel had walked—or rather lack of speed—spoke of a long recovery.

Guess you should've watched his Thanksgiving game after all.

———

Jahleel groaned as his eyelids tried to flutter open. The painkillers were giving him messed-up dreams. Visions of Oompa-Loompas and Whos dancing with Buddy the Elf lingered in his mind. He'd obviously watched too many Christmas movies lately.

Once more he tried to open his eyes to pull himself from the drug-induced nap. He sighed, thankful when the residual sleep slowly eked away. His eyes took in his surroundings. Pale blue walls. Football posters of Hall of Famers. Shelves lined with sports trophies.

Great.

Apparently some of his dream had been true. He was back in his hometown. Back in the bed he'd slept in for eighteen years. Of all the times to injure himself, it had to be during the Atlanta Falcons game, within driving distance of Peachwood Bay.

As he looked around the room, clarity returned, and he recalled the events leading up to this point. The doctors hadn't wanted him flying right after surgery, since his knee needed to be elevated as often as possible. So returning to Texas had quickly been crossed off his list of options. Since his parents had been watching the game when he made his glorious catch, they'd seen his dismal fall. And surprisingly enough, they'd rushed to the hospital in Atlanta. His mom had been waiting in his room the moment he was wheeled in from recovery.

At least the Desperados had beaten the Falcons.

A small grin appeared, then disappeared just as quickly. A win got the team one step closer to the playoffs, but now he lay here, sidelined by a blown-out knee. No way he'd be ready for the playoffs—or the Super Bowl, if the team managed to get that far—considering recovery was at least six months, if not longer. An ache filled his chest, and a ball of hurt filled his throat.

Why me?

The grandfather clock in the hall chimed. Jahleel glanced at his watch. *3:00 p.m.* Apparently the painkillers were more potent than he'd realized. The drive down the coast remained a blur. He sat up and groaned as pain radiated from his right knee. Had he sat up too suddenly? The immobilizer should have prevented him from jostling the injury. Instead, the brace weighed his leg down and added to the pain.

Jahleel willed his mind to ignore the hurt. Instead, he focused on the slight movements going on in his empty stomach. Food sounded good right about now. He searched for his crutches and frowned. *Who placed them beside the door?* They were at least nine feet away. What sense did that make?

Before he could complain, the bedroom door opened.

And the hits keep on coming.

"Good. You're awake."

Jahleel swallowed. There wasn't much he wanted to say to his father. The silence that had spanned between them over the last eight years had been wonderful. Carefree. *Guilt*-free. No one telling him to take up the mantle to preach because apparently a life of ministry was the *only* way Obadiah Walker believed his son could serve God. But if the

Lord gave Jahleel the talent to play football, wouldn't he be doing Him a disservice not to use that talent? The argument never persuaded his father, so Jahleel had stopped speaking in hopes his actions would back his words. Now he couldn't even achieve his Super Bowl dream this year.

He braced himself for his father's impending lecture. The man could write a book on criticizing a disappointing child.

"Your mama made some food. You feel like eating?"

"Yes, sir." Jahleel's lips barely moved as he aimed for a poker face.

"Good. I'll have her bring it in. You still like shrimp and grits, or is that too *common* for your taste?"

Hit one.

His father failed to remember that Jahleel had *never* looked down on his upbringing. He gritted his teeth. "That's just fine."

"Humph. We'll see how long that lasts."

Hit two.

His father walked out the door, not even sparing a backward glance.

The old irritation sparked at the slight. Jahleel could give in and feed the resentment or thank God that he wouldn't have to stay here forever. As soon as he got the okay to travel, he'd be on the first plane back to Texas.

Why had he let his mother talk him into coming home? Surely he could've found some hotel to lay up in while the swelling eased in his leg. Snippets of a conversation pressed on the edges of his memory. What had the doctor said? How long would he be off his leg? How long would he be beholden to Obadiah Walker?

Jahleel grimaced. He had the perfect reason never to step foot in Peachwood Bay again: his father. He had never measured up to the Reverend's standards. When he'd turned to football in junior high, their differences became starkly evident. Over and over Jay had been told how much time he wasted with a pigskin.

A snort escaped. His father hadn't even been satisfied when Jahleel earned a business degree before going to the NFL. First draft pick. Number one wide receiver for the San Antonio Desperados. Nothing pleased his father. *Nothing.*

A light tap sounded on his bedroom door.

"Come in."

His mother entered holding a tray of food. The smell of blackened shrimp wafted over to him. His mouth watered at the thought of the grits that would accompany the meal. Mavis Walker was famous for her shrimp and grits. Earned a blue ribbon year after year at the church showdown. The only other place a person could get shrimp and grits as good as his mama's was Sam's Shack. The diner served the best coastal Southern cuisine in Peachwood Bay. People actually drove in from a few towns over to enjoy the food.

Jahleel's shoulders dropped as the tension eased from the base of his neck. *Thank the Lord for moms.* His mother was the complete opposite of his father in every way.

"Brought you some lunch."

"Thank you, Mama."

Almond-shaped eyes resembling his stared back at him, filled with love and topped with blue eye shadow. Some things never changed. The thought lifted his mouth in a smile. Sure, a few more wrinkles lined her forehead and around her mouth, but the heart of his mama remained the same.

"You're welcome, baby." Her wide nose lifted with her smile.

The sound of her warm Southern voice soothed the bitterness that remained from his father's latest retort. She'd sounded the same when she fussed over past injuries he'd incurred growing up. In high school she never hovered, but as soon as he appeared hurt, she would be there, ready to soothe the ache with a meal and a hug or two.

He would never admit to anyone how much that had meant to him. Was that why his room had stayed the same? To welcome him home when he was ready to return? To prove she hadn't forgotten her only son? Or had his father forbidden her to come in and change it?

She placed the white tray over his lap and fluffed the pillows behind his back. "How's that?"

"Great, Mama." He squeezed her hand. "Thank you."

Just because he didn't want to be here, in this house, under his father's roof, didn't mean he'd take his foul mood out on her. She hadn't done anything to deserve an angry son. No, the fault had always been with his father. Jahleel started to say something and stopped. Why complain? It wouldn't fix anything or make a difference. He picked up his spoon.

"Don't forget to say grace."

"Right." He bowed his head and whispered a prayer of gratitude for the woman who could handle his father's bad moods *and* his. A twinge of guilt hit him. When was the last time he'd said grace?

"I've tweaked the recipe since your last visit."

He took a bite and moaned. The shrimp paired wonderfully with the cheese grits. He'd yet to find something like it in San Antonio. The best Mexican food: yep. Soul food: not so much.

There seemed to be an extra kick to the recipe. "Is it cayenne pepper?"

"Mm-hmm. You like?"

"Love." Spoonful after spoonful disappeared as his stomach warmed. "Too bad you didn't put my meds in here. Remember, you used to hide them in applesauce?"

"And you knew it. Every single time." She chuckled. "I can't believe you remember that."

"Ha! There's a reason I can't eat that stuff now. All I can think of is that chalky aftertaste."

20

"Then aren't you glad you can swallow them down like a big boy now?" She winked.

He shook his head, a smile on his face. "Man, the guys would rib me good if they heard how you talk to me."

"Please. I'm sure they would get a bigger kick out of your little reunion with Bebe."

Bebe? He froze. She was back in town? He hadn't seen her since before they both left for college. *You mean after you gave the whole "let's be friends" speech?* "What do you mean?" Caution slowed his words as nerves spiked his pulse rate. He set down his spoon.

"You don't remember?" His mother arched a drawn-on eyebrow in surprise.

"Please tell me I didn't do something stupid." *Not with Bebe. Anyone but Bebe.*

"You called her a 'fine Georgia peach.'"

Kill me now! "I didn't."

"Sure did. Hope got a kick out of it."

"Hope?"

His mom's head fell back, and a full-out belly laugh filled the air. She shook her head, her shoulder-length brown hair shaking from the movement. "Oh my goodness. I never thought some painkillers could be that powerful. Hope is Bebe's daughter. You asked her if she had a kid or a mini-me."

Jahleel let his head drop against the headboard. He didn't know what was worse, the fact that his mouth had gotten away from him or that Bebe Willabee had a child. Did that mean she had a husband too?

What does it matter? You ended the relationship, remember?

Jahleel licked his lips, searching for something to say to change the subject. To forget about a pair of pale green eyes that seared into his soul. His knee beckoned to him, ready to join the conversation. "I cannot believe I blew out my knee."

His mom's eyes softened. "God will heal you."

"Not in time for the playoffs. Plus, my contract is up for renegotiation." He wanted to voice the concern lurking in his heart but shoved it aside for another time. He'd wait to think about what was next after his physical therapist assessed the damage.

"God's got you, Jahleel."

More like He'd dropped him like a bad habit. Jahleel couldn't even blame God. His faith had taken a hit since he joined the NFL. Not because of anything bad. Plain ol' busyness had kept him from reading his Bible and from regular church attendance. Now he was suffering his first NFL injury . . . and probably a career-ending one at that.

I don't deserve Your forgiveness, but please forgive me. And if You could, please heal me.

Chapter
TWO

W hat do you mean he's back?" May's eyes widened. "You can't just drop that bit of information and then scurry away like a rat."

Bebe stopped in her tracks as her mouth dropped open. "A rat?" Not the look she was going for, but May wasn't wrong. Bebe didn't necessarily want to dissect all the ways Jay's homecoming was wrecking her.

"I knew that would get your attention." A mischievous grin curved May's mouth. "Is he still good-looking?"

Be cool, Bebe. "I'm sure some women would say so."

May had a tendency to sniff out any hidden subtext. Bebe tried to keep her body language nonchalant, but her heart beat too fast, ignoring her commands and causing her right eye to twitch.

"Ohhh," May whispered. "He's that fine?"

"May!" Bebe snapped.

"What?" Her black eyebrows rose in perfect innocence. Her ivory complexion and obsidian eyes completed the picture. May could be an Asian Snow White if it weren't for the freckles across the bridge of her nose, flaring onto her cheeks. She

23

flipped her straight black hair over her shoulder as she turned to doctor up a cup of coffee.

"We're in church, May."

She snorted. "Like God didn't already know the drool-worthy thoughts going on in your mind."

Bebe would laugh if she weren't half-mortified. Because she couldn't stop cataloging the ways Jay had changed from the high school senior who'd broken her heart. He'd been lean with muscle then, but now he was next level.

"We're Sunday school teachers," she reminded May primly. "Someone might hear us." Surely that would get her friend to change the conversation.

"Sunday school teachers who have a pulse." May took a sip of coffee. "I bet he's as divine as my cup of coffee."

Bebe chortled. Snorted. Then erupted in laughter. No way could she keep sense about her with May always dragging the juvenile side of her out. They'd been friends ever since May's family moved to town when she and Bebe were in the fifth grade.

Both of them had been different. Having a white mom and a Black dad had given Bebe a lighter complexion of brown skin complete with green eyes. May had been the only Japanese American in their class. All through their school years, they were both admired and picked on alike. Their differences had brought them together and cemented their friendship.

As their shared laughter died down, Bebe dabbed at her eyes with a napkin. Thank goodness she'd skipped the mascara and eyeliner this morning.

"Seriously, Bebe. He has to look better in person than he does on TV. Plus, he doesn't have all that equipment hiding his good looks."

"He was pretty loopy, which took the shine off his looks." *But not much.*

"Hmm. 'The lady doth protest too much, methinks.' Or

however that goes." May waved her hand as she took another sip of her drink.

"You said it right." Bebe walked toward the doorway, scanning the halls. *Clear.* She rejoined May. "Okay, I'll say this once, but let it be known it's not an admission of any kind of feelings. Just an admission of facts."

"Okay. Spill."

"He *is* better looking. It's totally not fair, but he is. No hint of fat anywhere on that man. And his arms look much bigger in person, although I'm not sure how, considering the camera should've already added ten pounds." Bebe scrunched her nose.

"It's a video camera, completely different properties."

Bebe rolled her eyes. She wanted to say his eyes pierced her soul and her heart went pitter-patter, but how could she when she didn't even want to admit it to herself? Jay had broken her heart after she'd spent months dreaming of a future with them together. She refused to fall for another man who couldn't go the distance, especially one who'd been the first to break her heart. "I was merely cataloging the changes time brought until he opened his mouth and called me a 'fine Georgia peach.' It went downhill from there."

May began coughing as she waffled between laughing and choking on her coffee. Bebe patted her friend on the back, shaking her head, then turned to fill her own cup once more.

"He did not say that," May gasped.

"Yes. Hope thought it was funny."

May's eyes widened. "She was watching? Wait, he saw her?" "Yes."

"And he didn't seem heartbroken that you'd obviously moved on?"

"Why would *he* be heartbroken?" It wasn't like he'd pledged his undying devotion in high school. That had only been her dream. "Besides, I'm divorced." Which still brought a bitter taste to her mouth. How had she been so expendable? Obviously something was wrong with her. Men never wanted to stick it out.

Why do I have such bad taste in men, Lord?

"Does he know you're no longer married?" May asked.

Silence penetrated the air. Even though others thought high school romances couldn't last, Bebe had believed they had forever power. Yet Jay's rejection and following silence indicated otherwise. After growing up next to one another all those years, for him to leave without a word . . . May knew exactly how much Jahleel's departure had destroyed Bebe.

Bebe shrugged. "Anyway, he asked how that happened." She relayed the rest of their meeting.

"Wow, those must be some great painkillers." May shook her head. "Did you see the replay of his injury on YouTube? It looked brutal."

"No, thanks." Bebe shuddered. Why on earth do people want to watch videos of others getting hurt?

"It was pretty fascinating. I'd love to get my hands on his medical charts."

"Rein yourself in, girl. He's not a science project."

"No, but my kids would love to study that in person. Especially since we're on the joint-and-socket unit."

Bebe shook her head. May was the high school anatomy and physiology teacher. Sometimes she laughed at how the two oddballs were now teachers. Though teaching certainly hadn't been Bebe's plan. That had come shortly after her marriage troubles with Will. Teaching allowed her to have the same school schedule as Hope, along with summers and holidays off, while providing a roof over their heads.

"Ladies, please get to your classrooms. People will be arriving soon."

May's face blanched at the sound of Reverend Walker's voice coming from behind her. Bebe nodded in assent, too unnerved to speak. How much of their conversation had he heard?

"Is he gone?" May met her eyes, whispering the question. "Yes."

Her friend slapped her arm before glancing around to verify the pastor was truly gone. "Why didn't you keep me from gossiping? You know the Rev walks the hallways looking for sinners."

Bebe chuckled. "I tried to remind you where we are."

"Hmm, likely story." May raised her mug in the air. "See you after service."

"Lunch at my place?"

"I wouldn't miss it."

Bebe headed down the hallway toward the five- and six-year-olds' room. Ever since she had Hope, being around children brightened her day. Well, really her whole week, since she taught kindergarten at Peachwood Bay Elementary. It seemed only natural to agree to be a Sunday school teacher for the church.

The classroom stood empty. She walked in, setting her cup of coffee on the front table. *I beat the parents. Thank You, Lord.* The children's tables were already covered with their morning warm-up activity of coloring. She'd set that up before getting something to drink. Today's lesson would focus on the star of Bethlehem that led the shepherds to the newborn Savior. Bebe inhaled as she thought of the coming Christmas season. This was her absolute favorite time of year. Nothing could bring her more joy than the birth of Christ.

Her thoughts drifted to Hope. Her darling daughter had been born on Christmas Eve, despite the fact that her due date wasn't until the first week of January. Bebe had gone into labor after catching her husband having a little too much holiday cheer with his coworker. Once upon a time, the memory would have dredged up pain and heartache. Now her heart rate didn't even change. Maybe it was a sign her prayers to forgive him were finally being answered.

As much as she had loathed Will at one time, Bebe could never regret the birth of her daughter. The only resentment she still struggled with was his current treatment of Hope. Like she wasn't worthy of his attention except for once a year at Christmastime.

Any day now, he'd mail Hope an early birthday card with money for her special day and Christmas. He never bothered to buy her a gift or even find out what she liked. Bebe shook her head, trying to lose the thoughts that threatened to drag her down. She would not let her mind spiral again. She'd place a smile on her face and greet each kid by name and remember the joy this season brought.

Her mind wondered back to Jahleel Walker. Would he still be at his parents' place once Christmas was over? And why did her heart quake at the idea?

Silence.

Jahleel sighed in bliss. His mother had hovered around him all yesterday evening, while his father glowered from his throne, the leather recliner he favored. He couldn't take the dichotomy between the two behaviors. But what else did he expect? His parents had been doing the same routine for thirty-two years now.

Jahleel snorted. This Christmas had the potential to be the worst one of his adulthood. Normally he'd throw a big bash, sparing no expense. His personal assistant would ensure a well-decorated tree graced his living room, perfectly situated in front of the floor-to-ceiling windows in his Texas home. All the guys from the team would show up with their plus-ones, and his current girlfriend would be in awe at the splendor.

Only this year was coming up *way* short. Jasmine had broken up with him in October. She'd apparently fallen in love with the Houston Rockets' starting point guard. If that wasn't bad enough, he'd found himself laid up and trapped back in his hometown. He couldn't do much but stare at the four walls of the house he'd been raised in.

He had offered to buy his parents a new place, but they had refused—most likely his father's objections. No matter how much money Jay made over the years, his father never accepted any monetary blessing from him. Obadiah Walker insisted on living below his means, as if the Lord would favor him more because of it.

Jahleel grunted. Being alone with his thoughts disturbed him. There was no escape. He never thought he'd return home, especially with an injury. Now he was beholden to the man who'd run him out in the first place.

"No son of mine is going to play football for a living. You should be glorifying God with a godly career," his father thundered.

"And how is using the talent God gave me ungodly?"

"You'll turn away from Jesus following this pursuit."

Jahleel winced. He hadn't turned away from his faith, but he certainly hadn't practiced it the way he used to.

Please forgive me.

His body practically vibrated with restlessness. Jahleel looked at his bookshelf, where his high school football rested. He'd caught three touchdown passes with that ball during his senior year homecoming game, leading the team to a win.

Gritting his teeth, he swung his right leg over the bed, the brace keeping it straight. If he could stand on his right foot and grab the football, he'd have some assurance that recovery was possible. That he could come back full-time to the sport he loved.

On a nod, he stood.

Pain shot from his knee, clawing against his skin. *Bad mistake.*

Sweat beaded across his forehead as he attempted to breathe through the pain. He should have taken pain medication an hour ago but had stubbornly skipped the dose. A puff of air escaped his lungs as he dragged himself back onto the mattress. His hands gripped his leg to ensure it wouldn't bounce.

Stars danced against his closed eyelids. Why did the pain have to be so intense?

Not worth it, Walker. Stick to the doctor's plan.

His chest heaved from the exertion. Slowly his breathing returned to normal while despair loomed. It was over. Kaput. Finished. Done for. He no longer had a football career.

Don't think like that. Wait until Ryan assesses you. But it was hard to look for the bright side when his knee throbbed this much.

The sound of the front door reverberated through the old walls, and he tensed. His parents were home already? He glanced at his cell phone. *Wow.* Service sure had ended quickly. He thought his father enjoyed pontificating in the pulpit for hours on end. Maybe the parishioners of His House Fellowship had finally revolted against long service times.

He sat still, waiting for his mother to come in and ask if he was hungry. He would lose muscle and gain fat if she kept it up. Especially since she kept offering all the mouthwatering meals of his childhood. Those shrimp and grits were still imprinted on his mind. Was that still Bebe's favorite meal?

His brow furrowed. Why was he even thinking of her? Their relationship had lasted the last half of their senior year and ended right before college. His scholarship to the University of Texas and her acceptance to Georgia Tech pulled them in different directions. Ending their romance had only made sense to him. He'd done the right thing, leaving and severing all contact. There was no way they would've survived the long distance . . . *right?*

Not that he had pined for Bebe. Sure, the memory of her soulful eyes sometimes tugged at him, but then he'd remind himself he'd done the right thing in breaking up. The statistics of high school sweethearts making it were pretty low. Obviously the fact that she had a kid meant she hadn't pined for him either.

She's probably married, proving your point further.

"Jay?" his mother called through the door. "You decent?"

"Yes, Mama." He ran a hand over his face. Had she knocked while he'd been thinking?

She opened the door, peeking her face through the opening. "We've got company. Make yourself presentable and come say hello."

"Company?"

"Yes. We always invite some people over after church. Surely you smelled that pot roast in the slow cooker?"

He could now that his door was open. His stomach rumbled in appreciation. "Could you bring me some food? I don't think I can walk."

"That's why you have crutches." She frowned. "You weren't walking without them, were you?"

He swallowed.

"Jahleel Hardheaded Walker."

"Could you please hand me the crutches?" He avoided her eyes, praying she'd ignore the need to lecture.

"Sure, baby." She grabbed them and brought them to him. "Brush your teeth and wipe your face. Then you'll be good as new." She beamed.

"I'm not a kid."

Her smile fell. "You're my kid."

"I'm sorry. I'll be right out."

"Good. Because Bebe's waiting."

The door shut, and his stomach dropped. How could he go out and face her, knowing he had made a fool of himself yesterday? Knowing she had a kid and probably a husband?

Suck it up, Walker. You're tougher than this. Except the crutches he held questioned that theory. *I could really use some divine intervention, Lord.* Hopefully his many prayers asking for forgiveness meant the Lord would hear his plea.

His exhale whistled as he made his way to the living room. Each step made him wince as he struggled to lean on the crutches and keep his weight off his injured knee. Served him right for trying to stand without aid in the first place.

Conversation reached his ears as he stopped in the doorway leading to the living room. A couple of people sat on the maroon sofa set, but most of the people stood in small groups around the open area. A nativity scene had been set up on one of the end tables flanking the couch. An angel graced the other. Not to mention the lit Christmas tree and garland hanging throughout the home.

His mother flitted from group to group, holding a tray of drinks, as soft strands of gospel holiday music filled the room. Jahleel scanned the room, noting the new faces and old. He stopped when he spotted Bebe talking to . . .

May? Did no one ever leave this town?

His gaze returned to Bebe like a magnet. Even from a distance, he could tell how petite her frame was. If memory served him right, she stopped growing at five foot three. As if she felt his gaze, she turned, and their eyes connected. Her pale green eyes glowed, and her hair fell in soft brown waves, brushing the top of her shoulders.

She'd grown even more beautiful, and Jahleel would've never thought that possible.

Bebe smiled and dipped her head in greeting. He lifted his hand in a small wave. May followed her friend's gaze, then smirked. She leaned forward and whispered something in

Bebe's ear. A blush graced his first girlfriend's cheeks, and she bit her lip, glancing his way.

What are they talking about?

It had to be about him. He wasn't being egotistical, but he was the prodigal elephant in the room. He began to hobble toward them. If they were going to gossip about him, he might as well listen to what they had to say.

Bebe's eyes widened, and her brow furrowed. She rushed to his side. "You don't have to crutch all the way over just to say hi."

Jahleel stopped moving. "What if I wanted to speak to May?"

"Oh." Her mouth dropped.

Why did he notice the little flecks of gold dancing around her irises? He blinked. "Uh no, not really. How've you been, Bebe?"

"Good." She wrapped her arms around her waist. "You?"

"Been better."

She winced. "Right. Sorry."

"What can you do?" He shrugged even though part of him wanted to shout, *Why me?*

"Eat your mama's bread pudding?"

Her Southern drawl dropped the *g* and added a lilt to the words, captivating him. He could always listen to Bebe talk, even about the mundane. She had this light and softness about her that had always drawn him in. But then they'd parted ways.

It was your choice. Own it.

Jahleel gulped and redirected his thoughts. "Bread pudding sounds good."

"Sit down and I'll get you some." She pointed toward the couches.

"You don't have to do that."

"Well, you sure can't." She motioned to his leg.

"Thanks, Bebe."

She waved it off. "That's what friends are for, Jay." With a smile, she headed for the kitchen.

Friend-zoned already.

But isn't that what you wanted?

He sighed.

Chapter
THREE

Bebe laid a hand on her stomach as she took a calming breath. *That's what friends are for?* She and Jay stopped being friends when he left for college without a backward glance. What were they now? Former classmates? Temporary neighbors?

Lord, please let his stay be temporary.

She needed a moment of reprieve from Jahleel Walker. He still made her feel off-kilter but no longer in a good way. Hopefully she could get his mom to bring him some bread pudding. Yet a quick scan of the room proved that to be futile. Mrs. Walker was nowhere to be seen. Maybe she had stepped into the kitchen. Bebe changed directions as memories of the past hounded her.

Jay's eyes had grown intense when she crossed the living room to join him. And after she asked if he wanted dessert, he'd studied her as if his brown-eyed gaze could see straight into her soul. Into the wounds that an uninterested husband and a divorce had caused. She couldn't remember the last time Will had really looked at her. His departure had left her feeling unworthy. Lacking. But Jay—well, one gaze had stripped away all her defenses.

Get a hold of yourself, Bebe. That path only leads to heartache.

Because as much as Jay pulled at her, Bebe would never belong in his NFL world. That had been the deciding factor in preventing her from contacting him when he went to college. She'd been hurt by his silence, but reminding herself they were on two different paths eventually eased the ache. He'd wanted fame and stardom, and she had wanted to be a counselor.

After meeting Will and having Hope, Bebe's dreams changed. Despite being married and having her own family, she could never bring herself to watch Jay's games. Thankfully there were thirty-one other teams to satisfy her love for football. Surprisingly enough, one could avoid one particular player if they had the will.

No one was in the kitchen, so Bebe dished up some bread pudding. The smell of the warm cinnamon bread and raisins tickled her senses. She lifted the ladle from a blue speckled pan and drizzled the pudding with the homemade cream sauce, staring down at the swirls. How was she going to go back out there and talk to Jay? She needed to be composed, show him she hadn't been thinking of him all these years later. But right now the heartache of *what-if* scenarios taunted her. If she didn't get herself under control, heartbreak would show all over her face.

He probably has a girlfriend. He is a star wide receiver, after all. Besides, you're not dating again. Remember what Will did to you? If he could cheat, what's to stop a famed NFL player from doing the same?

With a shake of her head, Bebe marched out of the kitchen and into the living room.

And stopped short.

Hope sat on the ottoman in front of Jay, a smile covering her face. Bebe couldn't see his expression, but Jay appeared enraptured by Hope's story, if the sound of his laughter was any indication. Hope continued speaking, using her hands to give life to her words. Bebe tried to gasp for air, but the picturesque moment felt like a punch to the gut. *This.* This was what her ex was missing out on. These moments of precious connection and precious time that he could never get back. Never.

Their daughter had never met a stranger. As frustrating as it was for Bebe to watch her talk to random people, she also didn't want to change the warmth that Hope often exuded toward others. Hope was the embodiment of compassion, and this time Jay was her target.

Bebe walked toward the seating area, wondering how she could extract herself and her daughter from the party. She didn't know how much her heart could take. To her chagrin, May had accepted Mrs. Walker's invitation for lunch for the both of them. Bebe had wanted to smack her friend with all the love and fury mixed inside of her. May knew how much Bebe wanted to avoid Jay and had taken fate into her own hands.

Or God had allowed her to.

Bebe looked around for her friend. *Nothing.* Knowing May, she'd probably snuck out and congratulated herself on a mission accomplished.

Resigned, Bebe offered Jay the bowl of dessert. "Here you go."

"Thanks." His warm gaze focused on her.

Shivers of awareness coursed up her arms. Had his voice always been so deep, or had time wrought changes? He appeared to be the boy next door she'd always known, but something in the depth of his eyes spoke of unseen changes.

"Mama, sit with me." Hope patted the ottoman.

"Honey, Jay needs to rest his leg on that." She was surprised he hadn't asked Hope to move. What if she accidentally bumped his knee?

"You could sit next to me." Jay winked as he patted the open space on the love seat.

She swallowed and sat down, hugging the end of the couch. Why was it called a love seat anyway?

Jay leaned over. "I don't bite, Bebe."

Maybe not, but he had the power to hurt her.

"Why would you bite my mom?" Hope had ears like a hawk.

Jay's face flushed, and he straightened. "I wouldn't. It was a joke."

"Not a very funny one."

Bebe's shoulders began to shake. She loved her daughter. She wanted to high-five her for lightening the mood.

"Mama, did you know Jay's a football player?" Hope's eyes glowed with excitement. Her daughter was a perfect mix of girly-girl and tomboy.

"I did."

"How come we never watch him on TV?"

Uh-oh. Heat filled her face. What could he be thinking? She glanced at him.

"Yeah, Bebe, how come?" Jay took a bite of bread pudding, amusement dancing in his eyes. "Don't you love football?"

"She sure does," Hope jumped in. "We bleed red and black!"

"The Falcons, Bebe?" Jay flattened his mouth in disgust.

"Like you didn't have a Michael Vick poster in your room growing up. Besides, we're in Falcons country. Who else would we root for? They don't play your games on TV unless y'all play the Falcons." He didn't need to know she had the sports package, allowing her to watch any team she wanted.

Hope's eyes widened. "Wait! You're the Desperados' wide receiver, aren't you? The one who blew out his—" She finally caught Bebe's look. "Uh, never mind." A sheepish grin graced her heart-shaped face. "I'm going to go play outside. 'Kay, Mama?"

Bebe nodded, although she wanted to call Hope back—or

anyone, for that matter. Why had May thrust her into this awkwardness? Did anyone want a reencounter with their ex?

She stood abruptly. "I'm going to go—" Words failed her as her hand found itself wrapped in Jay's warm one.

"Stay with me for a bit. Let's catch up?"

On what? The fact that her heart pounded like she'd just completed a record-breaking forty-yard dash? It drummed in her ears as his thumb ran up and down against hers. Memories resurfaced. Kisses under oak trees. Then a good-bye she hadn't seen coming. *Lord, please keep me from repeating my mistakes. I don't want to get hurt again.*

Yet with one gentle tug of her hand, Bebe found herself lowering to the love seat once more.

"There's no ring on your finger." Jay circled the place where one had once resided.

"I'm divorced." She licked her lips, wondering why her voice was so husky. "You?"

"Never married."

She didn't know how to feel about that. "Dating anyone?"

"Not currently."

Why did his answer light a spark? *Don't hope. Remember men are deceitful and walk away from the very first one who broke your heart.* "Huh, imagine that." Sass coated her words.

Jay dropped her hand and took another bite of his food.

Had she upset him with her indifference? *Why do you care?* Bebe cleared her throat. "How's the knee?"

"In pain."

"Have you been keeping up on your meds? You also don't want to dwell on the pain." She remembered how much it had hurt when she fell out of a tree at ten and had to wear a cast.

He arched an eyebrow. "There's not a lot to do when you're holed up in your childhood room, staring at old trophies to remind you that you're laid up."

"Wow, someone's throwing themselves a pity party."

Jay snorted. "You would too, Bebe."

"No, I'd make a change of plans." *Or move back home, heartbroken.*

"I can believe that." He stared at her, searching. For what, she didn't know. "Why did you come back?"

"My family was here. I got a job." Plan B, since Will had decided to break his vow of *forsaking all others*. She gestured toward his knee. "Have the guys checked on you?"

Pain filled his eyes so fast and then disappeared just as quickly. "A couple, but they're kind of busy. Hoping to cement the playoffs. I've already been placed on the injured reserve list." He sighed. "My contract is up for renegotiation, so I'm sure they'll forget about me soon enough."

Bebe stared at him, at a loss for words. She knew what it was like to realize your dreams were crashing around you. "I'm sorry, Jay."

One side of his mouth lifted in a crooked, self-deprecating smile. "Appreciate that, Bebe."

"So, what's Plan B?"

"Get through Christmas."

"What?" Why would anyone have to *get through* Christmas? Christmas was the best day of the year—really, the whole season lifted months of dreariness. Sure, Jay had injured himself, but that didn't remove Jesus from the throne. God was still good and worthy to be praised, worthy to be celebrated.

Bebe chuckled inwardly. She sounded like a walking advertisement for a religious conversion.

"Christmas isn't the same here as it would be in Texas," he said.

"It should be better. Your mom and dad are with you."

"Hooray." Only his voice sounded awfully sarcastic.

Jay leaned against the sofa cushion. The fact that he was with family *should've* put him in the holiday spirit. Instead, it utterly depressed him. His father's idea of a good Christmas was a long sermon at church pointing out the errors of every sinner's ways. At least, that was how his sermons went when Jay was a kid. If his father knew Jay had a tattoo on his chest, Obadiah Walker would have a coronary.

Jay looked at Bebe, wishing he could convey the depth of his misery being back here. "Bebe, you *know* how my dad is."

"I know he was a little hard on you growing up, but you're an adult now, Jahleel. Is it really that bad?"

He ignored the pleasure that spiked at the sound of his name on her lips. Tried to push the memory of the feel of her hand in his to the far recesses of his mind. Instead, he searched for the words. At one point, he could tell Bebe anything. Was that still the case?

He sighed. "Our last conversation didn't end on a good note. My dad hates my career and probably thinks I deserved to be hurt because of it. Or even thinks I was being punished. If it weren't for my mom, I wouldn't be here." *In more ways than one.*

Bebe bit her lip as she glanced toward his father and then met his eyes. "I'm sure he's missed you over the years. I think you'd be surprised by how much he's changed."

"If he missed me, why did he kick me out in the first place and tell me to never come back?"

Her pert nose wrinkled in dismay. He felt bad for putting her on the spot. His messed-up relationship with his dad wasn't her fault. His father had always been a little standoffish and more than a little judgmental. No need to focus on the argument that had led to his exile.

"No son of mine would enter the evil one's den."

"The NFL isn't inherently evil, just like all churches aren't inherently good."

He shook his head, trying to shake off the memories. He squeezed Bebe's shoulder and let go. "Sorry. Ignore me." He wouldn't dump his problems on her. No use repeating the past because he'd be walking away once his leg allowed him to.

"I'm sorry, Jay. At least you never have to question your mama's love for you."

A small grin formed. "Truth. Her love language is feeding me." He patted his gut. "She's going to make me fat. I wish there was something I could do to show her how much I appreciate it all."

"Just be here."

"I don't know how long I'll be here since Peachwood Bay is no longer home." He absentmindedly rubbed his right knee, frowning as he came in contact with the brace. He couldn't wait to get out of this thing.

"Jay?" Bebe's voice broke through his thoughts. She laid a hand on his arm. "Just try and enjoy your time with your folks. Remember how beautiful Christmas can be with family. How much joy you felt going to the boat parade."

"I almost forgot all about that. Does it still happen?"

Bebe nodded.

He let out a breath. "Okay. I'll try."

"Maybe you could come to church next week. Get out of the house and take in some fresh air."

"Kind of difficult to do with this leg." It hurt like the dickens, but here he was, posing for company for his parents' sake. "How can I prop it up there?" He glanced at her.

Her seafoam-green eyes studied his knee. If he knew her, she was plotting a way to fix everything. Bebe was a great friend. At times, he regretted how he ended things. He'd never had another friend like her since. *Or dated a woman like her.*

"Ask your father to get you a chair or something. He'll be so happy you're in church, I'm sure it won't be a problem."

"That's because he'll have another body to yell at."

Bebe chuckled. "He can be a little . . ."

"Judgmental? Fire-and-brimstone?"

"Stop," she whispered, lightly shoving him. "He hears everything. Just this morning—" A blush bloomed on her cheeks.

"Were you being bad in church, Bebe Willabee?" he whispered playfully.

"It's Gordon now, Jay."

"How fast we change the subject." His attempt at teasing fell flat because a shuttered expression came over her face.

"Self-preservation." She winced and stood. "I think it's time for me to go."

"Please stay. I don't know anyone here, Bebe." Why did he have to sound like he was begging?

"Puh-lease, Jay." She rolled her eyes, a hand perched on her hip. "Like anyone new comes to Peachwood Bay."

He tugged her back down. She huffed but leaned back against the cushion. "My friend Ryan's coming soon."

"Who's that? A teammate?"

"Physical therapist."

"He's coming to town? You don't have to drive to him?"

Jay stifled a chuckle. No reason to tell her he was rich enough to fly a therapist to his hometown. "He used to work with the Desperados before starting his own business. He's flying down as a favor."

"Not a free one?"

Jay shook his head. He forgot how quick-witted Bebe could be. "No, not for free."

"You plan on showing him around?"

"Where? It's not like we're jumping with things to do."

"Of course we are. It's Christmastime. If he's here in time for the boat parade, bring him. Or just take him to the beach."

The beach. It had been his and Bebe's favorite place to hang out. The hazy cyan hue of the Atlantic had seemed to settle around them, casting them in a bubble of seclusion.

"Jay?"

He blinked, bringing himself to the present. "Yeah, Ryan might want to visit. Just not sure if he'll want me walking around or out in the water."

"Water is good therapy." She squeezed his arm. "I'm going to head on out. See you around?"

"I'm not going anywhere."

"Bye, Jay."

He watched her walk away, reminded of another time, another place.

"Jay, we need to talk about college."

"What about college? You're going to Georgia Tech, and I'm going to UT."

Bebe stared at him, the wind blowing in her rich, brown hair. "How will we see each other? Do you want to keep in touch via email? Text?"

His gut clenched. How could he focus on college football if he had to focus on her? "We can use email to keep in touch." That wouldn't take up too much time. "After all, that's what friends do."

"That's all we are?"

"What do you want to hear from me?" His Adam's apple bobbed up and down. If she used the l-word, it would ruin everything.

Her green eyes darkened, and she stepped out of his arms. "What are we doing?" She gestured between them. "What is this? A f-fling?" The last word sputtered between her lips.

"Bebe. You know you're my best friend."

"You don't kiss friends, Jay."

But he couldn't help himself. Bebe Willabee was everything. Even now, the image of her on prom night dressed in a light green gown that had matched her eyes and shimmered like the sea tore at him. They could be more, but football . . .

"Bebe."

"So we're just friends, then?" She nodded slowly.

Some unknown emotion clogged his throat. "I . . ." He could do this. If he was going to make it to the NFL, then he needed to end their relationship. He didn't want to disappoint one more person. His father already expected him to fail. Jay didn't want to fail Bebe too. It was better to go back to being friends. "Yes. Just friends is all we'll ever be."

"How can you say that?" *A tear fell down her cheek.*

Because he had to. "It's better this way. You'll see."

And because he knew Bebe would never be the one to walk away, he turned and left.

Jahleel sighed, laying his head against the same sofa they had shared stolen kisses on. Why had he come back home?

Seeing Bebe brought up memories he thought were long buried. Only one glimpse at those beautiful eyes, and all he could see were his mistakes. He'd never emailed Bebe, and she'd never sent him one. Their friendship ended the day he walked away.

What if he had kept in contact? What if he had asked her to wait and be his girlfriend while he went to Texas for college? Would they still be together, or would he have disappointed her like he'd believed he would?

He ran a hand down his face, snuck a peek around the living room, and stood. It was time to retreat to his room and ignore the emotions Peachwood Bay was trying to bring out in him.

Chapter
FOUR

Bebe groaned as her cell phone rang. The simple ringtone belonged to one person: Will. She stared at the screen as it rang a third time. *Did she really have to answer it?* Another ring. *Answer or let it go to voicemail, girl.*

"Hello?"

"Lucille, it's Will."

She winced at the use of her given name. No one called her that. *No one.* Lucille was mere formality, and because her father was an avid B.B. King fan, he'd graced her with the nickname Bebe. Will refused to use her nickname, had thought it low-class. *Should've been red flag number one.*

"How can I help you?" *Please help me keep my cool, Lord.*

"I'm not going to be able to get Hope up here this Christmas. Angie's nonprofit is throwing a charity ball on Christmas Eve." He paused. "It's a black-tie event."

"You can take Hope with you. She'd enjoy it." Which was the truth. Her little girl loved parties and would love to get to know her father. She hadn't seen him since they moved here. Video phone calls once a year didn't count. And no matter how many times her ex chose Angie or some work event over

46

their daughter, her little girl refused to give up hope that she'd have a loving relationship with him.

Of course, it could be because Bebe refused to tell Hope about his annual request to see her. One he'd yet to follow through on.

"Ugh. It's like you don't even hear me. It's black-tie, *Lucille*. You know kids can't sit still at these types of prestigious gatherings."

He was *so* not a good person. How had she ever fallen for him? "Fine." She took a fortifying breath. "Maybe you could pick her up after the event. Keep her until New Year's."

"We'll be with Angie's parents. Their place isn't equipped for kids."

Why do I even bother? A picture of Hope entered Bebe's mind, and she made one last attempt. "She doesn't have to sleep over. I'd be happy to drive her up to Atlanta and occupy myself while you two visit." *Visit.* Her lip curled in derision.

"I'm *busy*. Don't you get it? You're the one with the time since you're a teacher." There couldn't have been any more derision if he'd put *teacher* in an online dictionary with the definition *useless*.

"Fine," she snapped. Why did she continue to try, year after year? He hadn't bothered to see Hope since the ink dried on their divorce papers. Even when they were married, Will had been away from home more than he'd ever been present. It was Bebe who'd attempted to keep their marriage together. She'd been so worried about being labeled a failure that she'd put up with way too much disrespect.

"Thank you." His words were clipped with annoyance. "Tell her I'll call her on Christmas."

"Her birthday is Christmas Eve, *Will*."

"I'll be busy helping Angie, *Lucille*. Besides, Hope won't care. Birthdays don't matter that much at her age. Bye."

She stared in disbelief at her mobile screen. How could he

think the day after Hope's birthday would be good enough? "Birthdays don't matter at her age? Do you even know how old she is now?" Her jaw clenched.

Lord, why does that man think he doesn't have to show up?

Bebe stared at her phone again, hot tears pressing against her eyelids. *How long will Hope have to pay for my mistakes?* She bit the inside of her lip and sniffed. Tilting her head back, she looked up at the ceiling. *Don't cry, don't cry.*

Three years. Three years since the divorce paperwork had been finalized. Almost eight years since he'd first cheated on her. Why had she stuck around after that? That should have been enough to send her back home right then and there. She was done shedding tears for herself, but her precious girl didn't deserve his indifference.

A knock sounded at her bedroom door. Bebe glanced at the clock on the nightstand. *9:30 p.m.* She blew out a breath, getting rid of any evidence of her sorrow even though Hope might notice anyway. Her girl didn't miss much. "Come in."

Hope peeked her head through the door, her little pink silk bonnet covering her hair. "Mama, I had a bad dream."

"Oh, baby girl, I'm so sorry." She patted the spot next to her on the mattress of her four-poster bed. "Climb in."

Hope ran and leaped onto the bed, grinning the entire time. Her gap-toothed smile pulled one from Bebe and made her wonder if her daughter really had a bad dream or just wanted some snuggles.

"Will you tell me about the wise men, Mama? And maybe I could sleep in here tonight?" Her doe eyes looked hopeful.

Bebe turned on her side, facing her sweet girl. "Just tonight."

"Yes!" Hope grinned, showcasing even more of her missing teeth. Seven was such a precious age. No longer a baby or toddling after Bebe, but not so grown that she distanced herself from her mother.

Whispering, Bebe told the story from memory. It was their tradition to talk of the men who searched for the Child King each Christmas season. Bebe painted a picture of a sky so dark but full of God's light. How the stars illuminated the darkness, but one in particular was their guide.

"A baby's a special thing, right, Mama?"

"The best, pumpkin." She traced a finger down Hope's face. Her cheeks had thinned out over the years, but that childish joy remained in her green eyes, ones that mirrored Bebe's own. *Lord, don't let her lose that joy in You.*

"But Jesus was extra special," Hope added.

"He sure was, and the wise men wanted to pay homage."

Hope's nose wrinkled at the word. Bebe used it every time she told the story, so her girl was used to hearing the difficult word. She just didn't understand why adults used big words when there were easier choices available.

Bebe picked the story back up, lowering her voice until Hope's eyes began to drift closed. Finally, she finished the tale. She closed her own eyes and sighed. *Lord, please let her remain full of faith, hope, and love. May she remember You are a perfect Father, even when her dad isn't. May she always remember the reason for the season. In Jesus's name, amen.*

Bebe stared at the Walker residence from her walkway. Candles glowed in the windows, and the simple white lights outlining the roof brightened the night sky. The wind danced through the trees surrounding the home, which gave the white lights in the trees the appearance of dancing. The porch light illuminated the front door as the porch swing swayed in the breeze. The house seemed to welcome her presence, but knowing who was inside had Bebe hesitating to go any farther.

She clutched the opening of her sweater. Any moment she'd gather the nerve needed to cross her patch of grass and step onto the Walkers' greener side. Tonight the church's Christmas committee was meeting with the Reverend and his wife to determine this year's holiday program. Last year was the first time they had deviated from the Reverend's tradition of a long sermon. Mrs. Walker had convinced him that times were changing and adapting to the younger crowd would prevent parishioners from leaving. The congregants were always restless when the Reverend decided to become long-winded, but Christmas brought out the worst—*or best?*—in him.

Last year, they'd separated the children from the parents for festivities. The kids had made Christmas ornaments: stars with Scripture written on them. After service, they'd held a potluck. Everyone had loved the turn of events—well, except for Reverend Walker. He'd stood to the side looking very much like Scrooge. She wasn't sure why he was so opposed to enjoying life, but considering the small population of Peachwood Bay, going to another church wasn't an option unless she wanted to travel out of town. However, he wasn't all bad. Bebe learned a lot from listening to his sermons, even when he went past the allotted time.

But that was neither here nor there. What she needed to do was place one foot in front of the other so that she could help plan this year's event. So what if she ran into Jahleel? Most likely he'd be holed up in his room.

Yet the idea of seeing him again made her feel like a watermelon with a thousand rubber bands squeezing it. An extra car had been in the Walkers' driveway when she came home from work yesterday, but now the car was gone. Probably Jay's physical therapist. Did that mean Jahleel had left as well?

Bebe glanced down the gravel road that served four other homes, all lit up with Christmas cheer. The Cavanaughs' home had the most decorations, ballooned Christmas figures filling their small yard. Bebe glanced back at her own home. She should put lights up this weekend.

Where was May? She'd promised to show early so they could walk inside together.

The front door of Jay's house opened. Mrs. Walker rested her hands on her hips. "Bebe, what on earth are you doing standing outside? Isn't it a little chilly for that?"

Praying God protects me from your son! She offered a strained smile. "Waiting for May."

"Humph. That child's never on time. Come on in here before you catch a cold."

Bebe sighed, tugging her knit cap lower. *You can do this.* Her short strides carried her across the yard and onto the Walkers' front walkway in a matter of seconds. *Short people are supposed to be slow walkers, Lord. I got here entirely too fast.*

Though it wasn't like the yard was that big anyway. Hadn't been when they were kids and certainly seemed smaller now that she was an adult. Strange to think of all the times she'd played in the yard with Jay while their mamas had looked on.

"Where's Hope?" Mrs. Walker asked.

"She's at Rosa's for a playdate." Thank goodness for the kindness of others. Since her parents moved to Florida last year, Bebe no longer had ready babysitters. Then again, she didn't go out much anyway.

"Oh, that's good. Come in, come in." Mrs. Walker motioned her inside, then quickly shut the white front door. "Barbara Ann is in the kitchen preparing some food for us."

"Great." Bebe gave a quick peek around the house, looking for signs of Jay.

"Jahleel's in his room getting cleaned up from his therapy session." Mrs. Walker smirked.

"How's that going?" Bebe kept a straight face, hoping not to give away any signs of embarrassment.

Mrs. Walker's mouth tugged downward. "I hate to see him in so much pain."

"I'm praying for him."

"Good." Mrs. Walker paused, cocking her head to the side. "How long has it been since you two talked?"

"We talked Sunday, remember?"

"No, Bebe. I mean really talked." The pointed look Mrs. Walker gave her sent flames up her cheeks.

She pulled her gray sweater tighter, wishing she could sink into a black hole. "High school." For some reason, she couldn't keep the truth from Jay's mother.

"Y'all need to fix this rift, or whatever it is." Mrs. Walker wagged a finger back and forth. "Y'all used to be the best of friends before . . ."

Exactly. Before she'd fallen for Jay and then had her heart trampled on.

"We're fine."

"Oh, really? Y'all used to talk to each other. *Every single day.* Then y'all go to college and act like you don't know one another. Uh-uh, something ain't right. Now, I'm not saying it's all your fault. I know how stubborn Jahleel can be. He is his father's son, after all."

Bebe let out a low sigh as shame filled her gut. She certainly hadn't tried to bridge the gap with Jay. Instead, she'd buried herself in college life. Then, when Will came along, her lonely heart had blossomed under his attention. Would she have fallen prey to his charms if she'd let go of the hurt and bitterness of the breakup with Jay? *Something to think about later.*

"Don't you worry. I'll give him a stern talking to as well. Just do your part, Bebe. You hear?"

"Yes, ma'am."

Mrs. Walker smiled, her brown eyes softening. "Good girl. Let's go sit in the kitchen. Obadiah is probably there already."

~

He would never play football again.

The pain of Ryan's words crushed him. If it had been anyone else, Jahleel would have called them a liar. But Ryan had always been straight with him. His Tennessee drawl had borne no nonsense with his assessment. He'd studied Jay's medical images and assessed the knee through touch. Instant relief had flowed through Jay's knee when Ryan removed the immobilizer from his leg. Unfortunately, standing had been its own ordeal. Ryan's goal was now to get Jay walking without a limp and to prevent any trouble with his left knee due to compensation. Apparently that was the best Jay could hope for.

It's not fair, God.

He should have had four or five more years before retirement even became a consideration. Plus, this was his very first injury—first major one, at least. You couldn't escape getting banged up playing football. Despite the uncertainty of his contract negotiations, his agent had assured him that getting re-signed was a done deal. Only now he couldn't even stand without pain and certainly not without the aid of crutches. Was he supposed to accept the fact that his career was over?

Laughter reached his ears. Had his parents invited more people over for dinner? Could Bebe be out there? The urge to hobble out of his self-imposed exile grew within him. If Bebe wasn't out there, no worries; he'd simply tell everyone he was hungry. If she was . . .

You'll what? Do you really think she wants to resume a friendship, considering how you ended things?

Maybe not, but Bebe was his only friend in Peachwood Bay. The only one he could be himself around and not expect censure.

Jahleel placed his crutches in position, rising on his good leg like Ryan had shown him. He could already feel a difference in his left leg. It didn't ache from the extra weight but accepted the load. Carefully, he headed toward the sound of laughter.

The glow from the kitchen cast a shadow on the hallway.

They must be in the eating area. The smell of fried foods drifted his way. Visions of hush puppies and catfish danced in his head. He hadn't eaten this much fried food since he was a teenager, back when he could eat all he wanted without worry of gaining weight.

He stepped into the all-white kitchen, and the chatter stopped. Everyone turned to look at him.

"What are you doing up?" Irritation filled his father's coal-black eyes. "Shouldn't you be resting?" Those words were a little softer than his initial question. Did his father really care, or was he pretending since they had company?

"I'm hungry." His stomach growled on cue. Thank goodness his cover became the focal point, because Bebe sat right at the table. *Huh. That's a new table.*

Her hair had been gathered into a ponytail. Instead of making her look plain, it accentuated her gorgeous heart-shaped face. And those eyes. The green depths had haunted his dreams since he'd returned home.

"Sure you are." May smirked.

"I can fix you something to eat, Jay." Ms. Barbara Ann smiled his way from her position in front of the stove.

"Thanks, ma'am." He ignored May's stare and her double meaning.

Ms. Barbara Ann gave him a side hug. "How's that knee doin', chil'?"

"It's a pain, but I'll live."

"To God be the glory." She pointed toward the dining table that fit eight people. "You want fried shrimp, catfish, or both?"

His stomach rumbled. "I'll have the catfish, please."

"Fries and hush puppies?"

He grinned. He'd been right. "Yes, ma'am."

"Good to know you didn't lose your manners in the NFL."

"He better not have." His mom chuckled.

Jahleel hobbled toward the end of the table. He stopped, searching for a way to prop up his leg.

"Here." Bebe stood. "You can use this." She pointed to her vacated seat. "Do you need a cushion?"

Movement in the corner of his eye caught his attention. His mom smiled, mouthing the words *thank you*.

"Thanks, Bebe."

"Sure." She walked out of the kitchen and came back with a pillow. Carefully, she lifted his leg and slid the pillow underneath it. "How's that?"

"Good." *Great.*

"We were talking about the Christmas program, Jay. Maybe you can stay and offer some suggestions?" His mom's eyes shined with hope.

"All right." He thought about what Bebe had said about enjoying the time with his parents. The least he could do was sit here and listen. Anything to make his mom happy.

She beamed and motioned toward his father. "Go ahead, Obadiah."

"Let us pray."

Jahleel peeked at Bebe while his father thanked God for their gathering. She was sharing a seat with May, eyes closed. He sighed and closed his own. *Lord, please help me remember I'm not staying in Peachwood Bay forever. No way, no how.* How easily he'd slipped right into praying again back home. *I hope that's okay, Lord.*

"Amen," his father said.

"Amen," they chorused.

"I hope everyone brought some fresh ideas with you for this year's celebration." His mom shot an extra-bright smile his way and then turned toward his father. "Obadiah, did you have any concerns before we brainstorm?"

His father leaned back in his chair and laced his fingers together, resting them on his stomach. "I think we need to remember this is the time to celebrate the birth of our Savior. I think the ornament craft and separate services for the children last year were a bit much."

"Oh, Obadiah. The people loved it." His mom looked around for validation.

"I agree," Bebe spoke up. "The kids had a blast last year, Reverend Walker. I think we should do something similar. All the ornaments had Bible verses, so the reason for the season was still honored."

His father nodded slowly. Jahleel was kind of surprised he didn't object further.

"What about a Secret Santa exchange?" Ms. Barbara Ann asked.

His father sneered. "Santa? Barbara Ann, you know how I feel about that."

"Yes, but the children love it. It doesn't have to detract from the Lord."

"Y'all need to stop lying to them." An air of disgust flew from his dad's lips.

"Calm down, dear," his mom whispered. "You promised."

Promised what? Jahleel watched as the others threw out suggestions left and right. He studied his father, noting the harsh lines etched in his forehead and the parenthetical ones surrounding his nose and mouth. However, the old man's frown made the most impact. Obadiah Walker detested change. Making ornaments sounded harmless, but it just might make the ol' man break out in hives. Still, his father remained quiet. Was that what he'd promised his mom?

Something May said started Jahleel's wheels turning. "What about a ball?"

"A ball?" His mom's mouth parted, excitement warring for attention with her blue eye shadow.

"A ball?" Bebe's pert mouth twisted. "What about the children?"

"A family ball. You could have a photo booth and everything. Surely those with kids would love the opportunity to memorialize it," Jay said, then waited for their opinions.

Shock flashed in Bebe's green eyes. Then . . . was that admiration? His pulse picked up speed.

"Absolutely not." His father slapped his hand on the oak table. "This is to revere the Lord, not dance the night away with booze."

"Obadiah, really!" His mother shook her head. "Jahleel didn't say anything about alcohol."

"I didn't, and there's nothing wrong with dancing."

"There's no place to host it." His father folded his arms across his chest.

"Rent out the town hall," May suggested. "We already have a decorating committee. They can make sure the town hall is up to par. Of course, the ball would come after your sermon."

No way would his father skip an opportunity to lecture.

"It's too excessive." His father shook his head. "That would cost a lot of money."

Like that was really the source of his objection. "I'll foot the bill." Jahleel stilled. Had he just said that aloud?

Everyone's head swung toward him like something from the movies. If there had been music, he was sure it would've lurched to a stop.

"What?" He shrugged.

"You'd foot the bill?" Bebe asked.

"Sure."

"The people of His House aren't a charity case." His father's bark rattled his ears. "We can contribute."

"You know what, that's a good idea." Jahleel looked at his father, stretching his mouth upward in a false smile. He'd never let the old man know his digs hit their mark. "We could make it a charity ball. I'll foot the bill for renting the town hall and anything else that needs purchasing, while the attendees can contribute an offering to go to a local charity of your choice."

"Oh! What about an angel tree?" Bebe looked around the table.

"That's a great idea," his mom said. "However, I'm sure those in need will need their gifts before Christmas. Maybe we make that separate from the ball."

Nods around the table met her comment.

"All in favor of a ball?" his mom asked.

Hands shot up around the room along with cautious glances toward his father. And it hit Jahleel. He wasn't the only one who disagreed with the Reverend's antics. Yet they all stayed and hung around him. Why?

Where else would they go when there's only two places of worship in town and the other is a Catholic church? Or maybe there was something more Jahleel was missing. Perhaps if he stuck around for the holidays, he'd figure it out.

Chapter
FIVE

They were throwing a Christmas ball. The irony wasn't lost on her. One minute Bebe was lamenting the horrors of rich men and their wallets, and the next she was planning a party with a rich man and his wallet. *A selfless one.* Okay, so the wallet couldn't be selfless, but Jay had certainly surprised her.

He even wanted the children to attend.

Be still her beating heart. It seemed Jahleel still had a caring spirit. With the passage of time, it was hard to know just how much of the boy she'd given her heart to in high school still existed. He'd always been so kind, and offering to fund the ball and talk of a photo booth showed that hadn't changed. He certainly was making it difficult for her to forget the good times and focus on the way he stomped on her heart.

She handed a bowl of ice cream to May, who was curled up on Bebe's gray sectional. Hope had already settled into bed, so it was a little quiet in the house.

"I can't believe the Rev agreed to a ball." May snorted. "Did you see his face when Jay suggested it? I thought he was going to have a coronary."

"I'm pretty sure he did once we left."

May winced. "You think he's over there ranting and raving?" She gasped. "Will he kick his son out again?"

Bebe licked peach ice cream off her spoon. "Is that rumor even true?" Never mind, Jay had mentioned it the other day.

"Of course it is. Gossip moves like lightning, and thanks to some people's attention to detail, the story elements all matched up."

"But how could he kick Jay out just because he went to the NFL? It makes no sense."

Bebe couldn't imagine doing something like that to Hope. Of course, she didn't want her daughter playing tackle football, with the high risk of injury that brought, but somehow she doubted that was the Reverend's concern. Growing up next door to Jay had shown her how harsh Obadiah Walker could be. He was a little blustery in his sermons too, but Bebe had never doubted his love for God. In the same way, she'd always imagined that Reverend Walker loved Jay no matter what. But did Jay hold that same belief?

"You know the Rev wanted Jay to be a preacher, right?" May's words came out more statement than question.

Of course. But Jay had never felt the call. "Well, kicking him out because he refused to follow in his footsteps doesn't allow the Reverend to throw a pity party."

"No kidding." May took a bite. "Why are we eating this? It's almost forty degrees outside."

"Outside, yes. But we're inside. Besides, you can eat ice cream any time of year."

"Hmm, I'm inclined to disagree with you, but this flavor is divine." May wiggled her eyebrows.

"You can't live in Georgia and not like peach ice cream."

"Somewhere there's a person who hates that flavor, but it's not me." May smiled as she shoveled a huge spoonful into her mouth.

"What am I going to do with you?"

Her friend shrugged as she dabbed at her mouth with a napkin. "Let's not talk about me. My life is firmly positioned in the boring box. You, on the other hand. . . ." Her voice trailed off, and her eyebrows rose in expectancy.

"My life is pretty boring too." Go to work with Hope, come home with Hope, sleep, and repeat.

"Not anymore," May sang. "Jay couldn't stop looking at you. I bet he was constructing soliloquies up there in his ol' noggin."

"He's a football player." Though he'd whispered pretty sweet romantic notions back in high school.

Stop thinking about then. Do you want a repeat breakup? Or even something that would lead to another divorce?

"With hearts in his eyes every time he looks at you."

Bebe smirked. May was a bit much at times but entertaining. "That's probably the haze of pain pills you see."

"No way. He looked much more alert at the meeting tonight." May looked down at her bowl. "How did I finish it so fast?"

"I did too." Bebe showed her own empty bowl. Temptation to lick it clean knocked. Instead she set the dish on the coffee table.

"Don't think I didn't notice the change in subject." May laid a hand on her arm. "I know you don't want to talk about him right now. You know where to find me when you're ready."

"Thanks, May." Bebe sighed. "It seems ridiculous to walk down memory lane just because he showed up next door. I mean, what do I actually think is going to happen?"

"That he'll knock on your door and ask you to take him back?"

Bebe chuckled. She couldn't help it. Before she met Will, that had been her exact wish. Then, when her marriage dissolved, she stopped thinking about the opposite sex for a while. Sometimes a guy at church would ask her out, or a tourist would show an interest. They'd all been so easy to turn away because she had no desire to repeat past mistakes. But none of them had the pull Jahleel Walker did either.

Did that mean she should seek closure? Find out exactly why Jay ended their relationship before they went off to college? Would that make it easier to avoid dreaming up what-ifs and keep her heart safe?

"You're overthinking, friend." May squeezed her hand. "It'll all work out."

"How do you know? Maybe this is just my hormones slipping into muscle memory due to his proximity."

"You're such a nerd." May tossed a throw pillow at her face.

"Likewise." Bebe retaliated. "Seriously, what do I do? Ignore him? Seek closure?"

"What do you want to do?"

I don't know! That was the issue. She felt bitterness, attraction, then anger at herself for being attracted to the man who'd broken her heart. "I think closure is the best track." She nodded to make sure her mind—and heart—thought of nothing else.

"Right," May drew out, then smirked. She stood, stretching her small frame. "Well, I'm out. I have some papers to grade before sleep beckons."

"See ya."

They headed outside, and Bebe clutched her sweater firmly to her. Why hadn't she grabbed her jacket? She flipped her hoodie over her head and sighed with relief. As long as her head was warm, the cold wasn't too bad. Plus, it would be gone tomorrow and in the low sixties.

Bebe waved as her friend's Honda headed down the road. She turned to go back inside and stopped.

Jay sat on his parents' porch swing, his long leg propped across it. He waved at her.

Closure.

Taking a deep breath, she headed his way.

Jahleel watched as Bebe drew closer. She still wore that ratty sweater around her like a shield. His mouth quirked. She'd always loved sweaters that were way too big for her. "Hey, Bebe."

"I cannot believe you suggested a ball." She propped her hands on her hips, her head cocked to the side in a look of amazement as she stood on the porch landing.

Neither could he. His father would hate his guts now. *And he didn't before?*

Feigning a nonchalance he didn't have, Jahleel cradled the back of his head and leaned against the swing back. "Everyone loves a good party." And maybe he wouldn't miss the one he'd normally throw back in Texas.

"Like children?" Her green eyes seemed to glow in the moonlight.

"Especially the kids." He could imagine Hope twirling in a Christmas dress and talking Bebe's ear off in the process. He held back a chuckle and focused on her face. He couldn't read her expression. Did she think the party should be kid-free? "You don't think it was a bad idea, do you?"

"I did until you mentioned letting the children attend." She leaned against the porch rail. "I'd hate for them to be left out. The whole congregation will love it. They really enjoyed last year's potluck." A soft smile brightened her face. "Plus, this allows us to dress up."

"Ms. Barbara Ann still wear those huge hats? Looking like she's going to the Derby?"

Bebe's soft laugh blended perfectly with the atmosphere. "Of course. You should have seen last week's. It looked like a birdbath."

He laughed, leaning forward to catch his breath at the image. "I can only imagine."

"Maybe you'll luck out and she'll wear it again." Bebe snickered.

Jahleel shuddered. "I hope not. I won't be able to keep a straight face."

"Hope can't either."

Hope. It seemed a shame that little girl didn't have a father around. He stared at his childhood friend. "What happened with Hope's father?" *Please don't deflect.* Maybe he shouldn't try to connect with her again, but he couldn't stop himself from caring and wondering what all he'd missed out on since their last parting.

Silence filled the air. Just when he thought she would ignore his question, she shifted against the porch rail. "He didn't want me anymore."

The smallness of her voice gutted him.

Bebe opened her mouth and then shut it. Did he even want to know what she'd been about to say? Because the situations were too close for comfort. It wasn't that Jay hadn't wanted to be with her. He'd just had other priorities.

Ouch. That's worse. How had he been so self-absorbed?

Aren't you still?

"I'm sorry, Bebe."

"Not your fault."

This time. But had he given her the impression he didn't want her when he left for UT? He rubbed his chin. "How does Hope deal with his absence?"

"With optimism. The disappointment never lasts long. Though I'm not sure if that's a good or bad thing." She picked imaginary lint off her sleeve.

"Does she get to see him at all? Talk to him?"

"No. Well, once a year. She talked to him last Christmas."

"Wait, what?" His emotions teetered between rage and sorrow for the joyful little girl. "Why? How can he *not*?"

"He's busy with his new wife, Angie. They head multiple charity organizations." Bebe rolled her eyes.

"What about his own child?"

Bebe blew out a breath. "I tell Hope that God is a father to the fatherless. I don't think she understands exactly what I mean, but I'm hoping the seeds will be planted and it'll keep her from becoming bitter as she grows up. At least she'll remember God was always there."

"Oh, Bebe."

"Don't sweat it, Jay."

Silence fell between them as he studied the girl next door. He'd always been able to tell how Bebe felt. Their communication had flowed freely up until he decided to cut all ties. All he could think of right then was how much of a mess he'd made when they broke up. How did you keep yourself from thinking what-ifs and wanting to kick yourself in the rear?

"Could you sit down so we can talk?" He gestured to the inordinately long porch swing. He pulled one of the ottomans from beneath the swing and propped his leg on it.

Bebe stared at him and then the swing. With a small sigh, she crossed the porch and carefully sat down. He couldn't help but appreciate the care she took not to jostle his leg.

She sat with her hands folded primly in her lap. Now that she was near him, he didn't know what to say. *Sorry I was a jerk? Sorry I couldn't be who you wanted me to be?* Nah, that just negated all responsibility.

"I don't plan on freezing all night, Jay."

"Then scoot on in." He lifted an arm, knowing she wouldn't come any closer.

"Uh-uh." She waggled a finger at him. "Just state your piece."

Jahleel ran a hand down his face. *This is Bebe. Be honest.* "I'm so sorry I was a jerk the last time we talked."

"We were kids, right?" She shrugged as if to insinuate it no longer mattered.

That was her putting on a brave face. Bebe felt deeply, and he had no doubt she still harbored some resentment. After all, if she didn't, they'd be talking much more freely.

"I don't think either of us thought our feelings childish. Besides, that doesn't excuse my behavior. You wanted to know how we were going to maintain contact going off to different colleges, and I shut you down. I shut *us* down." His throat dried. "I feared I wouldn't be able to focus on football, on obtaining the NFL dream, if I had a girlfriend."

Sorrow filled her green eyes. "You were my best friend before you were my boyfriend, and you just cut off all contact." Her eyes watered. "Why? Was I that bad of a girlfriend—"

"No," he said forcefully. "It truly wasn't you but me." He pointed to his chest. "I didn't know if I could have both dreams, Bebe. So I chose football." He winced. Great, he'd just told her he picked a sport over love. He blew out a breath. "I'm sorry for not being the friend you needed. And definitely for not being the boyfriend you deserved."

Tears spilled down her cheeks, and his gut clenched. "I might have been able to forgive the boyfriend part, Jay. But for you to just ignore me. . . ."

He wanted to pull her into his arms. He could feel her pain as if it ached in the center of his own chest, as if it were his own. And maybe it really was. He was finally admitting what he had let go. And for what? A sport he'd no longer be able to play?

"I was a class A jerk. Please forgive me," he whispered. Acting on hope, he slid closer, draping an arm around her shoulders.

She laid her head on his shoulder. They said nothing for a few moments. Jahleel prayed God would heal any hurt he'd inflicted on Bebe.

Finally, she shifted away and met his gaze. "I forgive you, but this"—she pointed between them—"isn't a good idea. We went down that road and saw the dead-end sign."

Jahleel nodded, trying to swallow around the knot in his throat. The thought of closing the door to something more kind of tore him up inside. It would be so easy to lean forward and kiss her soft lips, remembering all the reasons Bebe had always had a place in his heart. But staying in Peachwood Bay wasn't the plan. It would be more shades of the same bad behavior if he started something again. This time around, he needed to be more responsible and respectful.

"Friends?" He licked his lips, hoping to cover the crack in his voice.

"Friends." She held out a hand.

He squeezed it and promptly let go. No use lingering.

Bebe leaned against the back of the swing and curled her feet underneath her. "Now, bring me up to speed on your life."

So he did, all the while wanting more. But how much of himself was he willing to give?

Chapter
SIX

JAY

We're friends, right?

BEBE

That's what we agreed to last night.

JAY

My mom is driving me crazy. Can I come over, friend? I promise not to bug you.

BEBE

If you come over, I'm putting you to work.

JAY

What are you working on?

BEBE

Baking Christmas cookies.

JAY

Bet. I'll be right over.

Well, as soon as these crutches let me.

Bebe set her cell phone on the countertop. A soft sigh escaped her lips as she remembered the warmth of lying on Jay's shoulder Tuesday night. She'd felt a chink in her armor at the closeness but had managed to remember forgiveness didn't mean forgetting. Bebe was all too happy to have walked away unscathed by memories or the attraction that hadn't been erased by time. Maybe it was a Christmas miracle.

"Jay's going to come over and help us bake," she told her daughter.

"Awesome." Hope clapped her hands. "Do we have a football-shaped cookie cutter?" she asked, her eyes wide.

"I don't know, sweetie. We *are* making Christmas ones, though." Bebe pointed to the cutters in the shapes of a Christmas tree, stocking, candy cane, snowman, and gingerbread man.

"Yes, but football season still goes through Christmas. Plus, Mr. Walker is a football player."

Bebe loved that Hope was respectful by calling him *mister*. She also loved how her daughter wanted to make cookies that meant something to Jay. God willing, he would take the olive branch and not be offended, considering the Desperados placed him on the injured list.

"Go see if we have one in the cookie cutter bin," Bebe instructed.

"Yes, Mama." Hope scurried off, quickly searching through the plastic container that held all the cookie cutters. "Found one." She held up the offering, a big smile on her face.

"Great."

The doorbell rang.

Bebe wiped her hands on a towel and went to the front door. She opened it and took in the sight before her. Jay had on a UT sweatshirt and black joggers. A weary look drew his mouth down.

"She's hovering, huh?" Bebe asked quietly.

69

"Too much. Between her asking me if I need anything every five minutes and my dad grunting with disapproval . . ." He sighed. "I just needed some fresh air." He sniffed. "And cookies smell a whole lot better than parental shame."

Bebe chuckled. "Christmas cookies make everything better."

"You're determined to bring the Christmas spirit, aren't you?"

She smiled. "Jahleel Walker, I know you once loved Christmas as much as I still do. Your current Scrooge state is because of the company you keep, not the holiday season. So come on in, listen to some holiday music, and make football-shaped cookies."

"Football cookie cutters?" His eyes crinkled as his lips curved upward. "That Hope's doing?"

"How'd you guess?" She stared at him curiously.

He tapped the side of his temple. "I knew."

She wasn't so sure if Jay really did know or if that was simply a lucky guess. Nevertheless, she led the way to her kitchen. Her gaze flitted left and right as she mentally tried to figure out just how Jay could perch on a barstool to help without aggravating his leg.

"I'm not so sure this will work," she mused out loud.

"Don't worry about me. I'll see Ryan later, and he'll work on my knee. An hour or so sitting here won't kill me."

She met his warm gaze. "Are you sure?"

"Yeah." He sat down, then looked at Hope. "Good afternoon, Miss Hope."

A demure expression filtered across her daughter's face. "Good afternoon, Mr. Walker." She held up the cookie cutter in his honor. "This is yours. You can cut out as many as you want, but make sure you get some good Christmas ones in too." She nodded once as if to dot the end of her speech.

"I can do that." He looked around Bebe's house. "Where are

the decorations? I thought you'd be all decked out, as much as you talk about the love of Christmas."

Bebe sighed as she took a Christmas tree cutter and began to make cuts in the rolled-out dough. "It's on my list to do this weekend."

"We should decorate tonight," Hope exclaimed. "We have help now. You do want to help, right?" She stared at Jay expectantly.

"I'd love to." He smirked at Bebe. "Do you want my help, *friend?*"

She knew exactly what he was doing. Yet seeing his friendly expression with that hint of teasing didn't churn her stomach into knots. No, she actually felt like they were friends again. For some reason, Bebe had to battle against tears at the sweet thought. *I missed this.*

She turned away, clearing her throat. "Sure. That would be helpful . . . *friend.*"

Nothing more was said as they listened to Toni Braxton sing "Have Yourself a Merry Little Christmas." Bebe looked around the kitchen island, and her breath caught. Hope had a look of pure concentration as she switched out different cookie cutters. And Jay—well, Jay was staring right at Bebe.

Her cheeks warmed, and she averted her gaze to the cookies. "Guess I should get some of these in the oven."

"Will you ice and decorate them when they've cooled off?" Jay asked.

"Mm-hmm." *Why was it so hot in here all of a sudden?*

It wasn't like she'd never seen a man staring at her. In fact, she'd caught Jahleel looking at her many times before. *Yeah, in the past. But y'all have moved on from that. You're here now, in the present, and that wasn't a look you give a friend.*

She swallowed. But they'd already agreed nothing would happen between them. They'd stay in their lanes—individual lanes, of course—and when he went back to Texas, that would be that.

Her heart would be completely safe because there was no romance brewing. How could a person fall while making cookies?

You can't. You're just doing a festive activity to help him see the joy of Christmas once more.

Right. Feeling better, Bebe put the first batch into the oven and set the kitchen timer.

"Okay, should we decorate the house while the cookies bake?" she asked.

"Yes!" Hope squealed and jumped up. "I know where the bin is. I'll bring it out."

"It might be too heavy, Hope."

"Then I'll push it, Mama." Hope rolled her eyes as if annoyed by Bebe's obvious lack of common sense.

Instead of being offended, Bebe chuckled. She turned to Jay. "Want to sit on the couch and get that leg elevated?"

"How can I help decorate if I'm sitting?"

"You can hand out the ornaments. Make sure nothing looks crooked."

He nodded. "Okay. I'll be the DJ as well."

"Hey, what's wrong with Toni Braxton?" She placed her hands on her hips.

"'This Christmas' by Chris Brown is better. I mean, he even starred in a Christmas movie."

"Okay, I like that song, but Toni is classic. Who doesn't like her voice?"

"Maybe the rest of us know there are other artists besides her." Jay gave her a mock-exasperated expression. "Besides, shouldn't you be listening to the blues?"

"Not for Christmas," she sing-songed. She sat on the couch next to him. "Actually I only listen to the blues when I miss my folks."

"I can understand that. Will they visit for the holidays?"

She nodded. "Yeah, they wouldn't miss their time with Hope."

"I look forward to seeing them again."

Her folks had always liked Jay. Her mom had been confused when he left for college and just stopped talking to Bebe. Eventually, she stopped asking if Bebe had heard from him. "They'll like that. My dad's been praying for your recovery."

"I appreciate that." His brow furrowed. "I'm not sure I'll—"

"I've got them," Hope yelled as she pushed the bin into the living room.

Bebe jumped up to help her. They could put the tree right in front of her picture window, which was catty-corner from the couch. The stockings would go on the faux mantel—no fireplace—and the nativity sets she owned would be strategically placed on the mantel.

"Where's your tree?" Jay asked.

"Oh, yeah. I saw that. I'll grab it," Hope said.

"We have an artificial one." Bebe shrugged. "I know it's not as popular as cutting your own, but it saves on pine needle cleanup."

Jay laughed. "I'll say. I think a lot of people are moving to artificial trees now for various reasons."

Why did his lack of censure warm her? Did she really think he'd judge her for going artificial versus the real thing? *Will would have.* Oh yes, her ex-husband always required a real tree when they'd been together.

Bebe shook off the gloomy thoughts. "Hmm. I never see a fake tree in a Hallmark movie. They're always chopping down their own trees."

"Yeah, when the big-city woman goes to a small town and meets a farmer who needs help? Of course he's chopping down trees. How else can they throw in a plaid-wearing ax scene?" Jay smirked.

She laughed. "Make fun all you want, but I love those movies. Besides, it's not always a small-town guy versus a big-city heroine. Sometimes it's the other way around. Or sometimes they're childhood nemeses who pair up to save Christmas."

Bebe held in a gasp. Would that be her and Jay's story this season? Two high school exes who had to work on the Christmas ball and bring joy to the people of Peachwood Bay?

She blinked, then snorted softly to herself. This was no Hallmark movie. Besides, she could think of only one holiday movie with a football star. Nothing in her situation matched that.

You're good, girl. Push these romantic notions aside and remember what's at stake. Your heart. Will trampled it, but before him was Jay. Forgiveness doesn't necessarily equate forgetfulness.

If Bebe could remember that fact, then she would make it through the next few weeks just fine.

Jay could see the wheels turning in Bebe's beautiful head. Something about their conversation had sent her into think mode. If she was anything like she'd been in high school, she'd either worry the subject to death or shake out of it and worry another time. Was it wrong for him to want to study her and figure out which choice she'd pick?

"Mama? Will you help me put the tree together?" Hope asked.

Bebe grinned, seemingly shaking off her thoughts. "Sure, sweetie."

Jay grimaced. Surely he could put a tree together without making anything worse for his bum knee. "Bebe, why don't you bring the parts over here? I'll put it together."

"I don't know," she said skeptically.

"Trust me. I got this." He had *no* idea if he did, but he wouldn't admit that to her.

"Let him help, Mama."

Bebe nodded and slid the tree pouch over to him. Jay picked

another Christmas song, then started connecting the pieces together. Hope giggled as she followed her mother's instructions to hang up four stockings. He could read the names of Hope, Bebe, and Bebe's folks. Once more, his thoughts turned to Hope's missing father. How could he leave someone like Bebe and someone as adorable as Hope?

Didn't you leave Bebe?

He winced. Though she'd forgiven him, Jay couldn't help but feel like he had to make it up to her somehow. But how?

Maybe enjoy Christmas like she's been urging you to. After all, it was his favorite time of year. If he was in Texas, he'd have no qualms about celebrating it as much as possible, party after party. But seeing his dad and how quickly disapproval rolled off him made Jay pause. As if he was afraid celebrating the holiday would incur more censure. Experience had taught him the only way Obadiah Walker observed Christmas was by reading his Bible and reminding folks that this was a made-up holiday based off of paganism. No matter how many times Jay tried to show redemption in the way people focused on the Lord more, his father refused to see a different perspective.

Maybe that was one reason he suggested the ball, just to see how his father would react. Seeing the rest of the church committee back him hadn't been something he thought would happen. But it felt good knowing they wanted the ball just as much as he did. Could God somehow work a miracle and change his father's heart?

"You done with that?" Bebe asked.

"Yeah. I fluffed the branches as much as possible." He winced as she tried to right the assembled tree. "You need help?"

"No. Stay seated."

He held back a sigh. He'd wanted to escape his mom's hovering, but now he'd put himself in a position of feeling useless.

Bebe got the tree into the stand, then stood back and smiled. "This is going to be great once it's lit."

"You got one with colored lights?" he asked.

Her eyes widened. "How did you know?"

"Come on, Bebe. You always loved the houses that decorated with multicolored lights versus plain ol' white ones. You haven't changed *that* much, have you?" He held his breath, waiting for her answer.

For some reason, he needed to know Bebe was still the same. Still full of light, kindness, and love for her neighbor. Being around her had always brought him comfort. Was that what he was seeking now?

"I've changed but not in that area." She tilted her head. "What about you? Do you still go for all-white lights at Christmas?"

His neck heated. "Maybe," he replied slowly. In fact, his mom had started that tradition. He guessed he'd kept something of Peachwood Bay after all.

She tilted her head back, laughing.

"What's so funny?" Hope asked, looking back and forth between them.

"Your mama has horrible taste in Christmas décor." Jay smirked.

Hope feigned a gasp, clutching invisible pearls. "But the colored lights are the best!"

"They're not horrendous," he conceded.

Hope squinted. "And what are your feelings on nativity scenes?"

"Is it really Christmas without one?"

"Good answer," she mumbled, sounding like a woman a lot older than seven.

Jay stifled his laughter and glanced toward Bebe, who looked like she was doing the same.

The timer beeped, and Bebe went into the kitchen, exchanging one cookie sheet for the next. She hummed to herself as she placed the fresh cookies onto a cooling rack. Would this have been what their life looked like if he hadn't cut ties before college? Would he and Bebe have gone the distance and lived a life celebrating the Lord all year long, not just for the holiday season?

He looked at Hope, looked at Bebe's cozy home, and felt nothing but regret. Maybe his father was right. Jay had chased football, forsaking all others. He didn't think playing football was a sin, not at all. *But did you make it an idol?*

Jay cleared his throat. "Those cookies ready to ice yet?"

"Of course not." Bebe shook her head, amusement dancing in her eyes. "They've got to cool."

"Maybe I should taste one to make sure they're worthy of icing."

"Oh, me too, Mama. We wouldn't want to frost bad sugar cookies," Hope chimed in.

Jay held out a fist for a bump. The little girl immediately crossed the room to give him dap. "My kind of kid."

Hope beamed, showing off her missing front teeth. Yeah, Hope Gordon was an adorable kid, and her father was definitely missing out. Maybe Jay would make sure to come over and hang out with the two Gordon women so they weren't lonely this Christmas season.

Yeah, I'm sure you're thinking that out of the kindness of your heart.

Obviously it had nothing to do with the fact that Bebe lightened his burdens and made him feel peace. And maybe, just maybe, she could help him enjoy this Christmas.

Chapter
SEVEN

The sounds of "Blue Christmas" accompanied Bebe as she drove down the road toward His House Fellowship. The stress of the day drained away as her body relaxed against the driver's seat, her head weaving to the music. The atmosphere in the car made her want to rush home and turn on the Hallmark Channel. Besides celebrating Jesus's birth, she lived and breathed Christmas movies. Thank goodness she had the streaming app to watch all of them.

Her mind flitted to Jay. Decorating her house and icing the Christmas cookies with him and Hope had done something to her heart. It was like a part she hadn't known about had received healing and felt the balm of a friendship. The joy of the time together had quenched places that had been far too dry in her heart. Now all she had to do was remind herself why engaging any romantic fancies was a very bad, no-good idea.

Her mind shifted as the white steeple of the church loomed in front of her. It reached for the heavens, and the point disappeared into an overcast sky.

Please don't rain. She didn't have an umbrella and especially hated driving in wet weather. The streets of Peachwood Bay quickly morphed into red sludge with the slightest hint of precipitation.

There were only a couple of cars sitting in the church parking lot when she turned into it. May's red Honda sparkled in the front row, a few spots down from the Reverend's vehicle. Who knew May would beat Bebe here? She chuckled softly. May was probably climbing the walls, wishing for someone to help keep her from having to talk to Reverend Walker.

Bebe grabbed her monogramed tote—a gift from a student the previous year—and headed inside. The warmth of the vestibule enveloped her as the double doors closed behind her. Strands of the "Hallelujah" chorus from Handel's *Messiah* washed over her as she stood in the hall.

Reverend Walker loved classical music. He was convinced it was God's music. Personally, she liked all music, but she had to admit, walking into the sanctuary with stringed instruments serenading her made her think of the pearly gates and angels singing to the Lord.

She turned and headed down the side corridor, toward the back of the building where the conference room was situated. She removed her gloves and kept walking, stuffing them into the tote. A nudge cautioned her, and she slowed, looking up at the same time.

Jay.

Nerves made her stomach dip up and down as if she rode a Ferris wheel at the state fair. He wore a tracksuit, his knee brace firmly supporting his leg while his arms clutched his crutches. Why did he have to look so good in something so basic?

So he's handsome. Acknowledge the fact and move on.

"What are you doing here?" And why was she excited to see him? Had time spent with him yesterday turned her into a woman who felt a pitter-patter at just his presence?

No, Bebe. You're friends. Be cool.

"Mom asked me to attend the committee meeting since I offered to foot the bill."

Oh. "Makes sense."

His pale pink lips curved upward. "Plus, I wanted to hang out with my friend."

Friend. She blinked. "Do you need me to find you a chair to prop up that leg?" She slowly moved forward, disappointment tugging at her. But why? They were good at being friends. Wasn't she just thanking God for that a moment before?

"Nah, Mom has that covered."

"Okay." She bit her lip. Now what?

Jahleel gestured toward the conference room. "Come meet my friend Ryan."

"Who?"

"My physical therapist."

Right. "You brought your therapist to the committee meeting?"

He shrugged. "He wants to make sure I don't overdo it. Come on."

She matched Jay's pace. When she entered the conference room, she stopped short. May sat across from a tall, white gentleman, and she was . . . giggling? Bebe's mouth dropped open in shock. Never had her friend exhibited such a giddy façade. It was a bit unnerving.

"I feel like I just walked into a horror film," she whispered to Jay.

His chest shook with suppressed laughter. "I admit I didn't expect to see those two connect. Ryan hasn't cheesed this much since . . . ." He shrugged.

"So, what, they just decided they like each other?" Life was not that easy.

"It's easy for some people." Jay met her gaze.

Stared.

Seared into her being.

"Jay," she breathed out.

"I know, Bebe. We can't go backward."

But at the moment, she wanted to. She shook her head. "Why don't you introduce me?"

"Right." He rubbed the back of his neck and then grabbed his crutch.

She followed him while examining May. Her friend's face flushed pink, and her freckles seemed to have deepened to a golden brown. Jay cleared his throat, and May and the therapist whirled around, surprise on both their faces. Had they forgotten they weren't alone but in a room full of people?

"Hey, Ryan, this is Bebe. Bebe, my friend Ryan."

"Nice to meet you." He offered a hand.

"Likewise." She shook it, glancing at May out of the corner of her eye. Her friend looked down and began picking at some tape on the table. Bebe slid into the seat next to May. "Your cheeks are flaming," she murmured.

"Shh. Like yours don't around Jay."

Touché. Before she could finish her retort, Mrs. Walker and the Reverend walked in. The rest of the committee quickly followed, and introductions were made.

They sat down, and the Reverend folded his hands across his stomach. "I've decided not to continue on the committee." He looked at his wife. "Mrs. Walker pointed out that my time is needed to reflect on this year's message."

Thank You, Lord. Bebe didn't mean it maliciously, but the meetings would be less tense if he didn't participate. She sent a small smile of gratitude toward Mrs. Walker. The older woman winked in understanding.

"All I ask is that you remember why we're celebrating. No need to be outrageous." His last words seemed to be directed toward Jay.

Bebe wanted to lay a hand on Jahleel's arm, but he sat across from her. His face remained impassive, not a hint of his thoughts showing. Did the subtext the Reverend hinted at bother him? *Of course it does.* Bebe had to remember to be gracious toward Obadiah Walker. Despite his bluster, she'd learned many things from him that had helped her faith. He wasn't all bad, more like a curmudgeon in those Christmas movies who needed his heart to grow.

"I'll take over from here, Obadiah." Mrs. Walker kissed her husband on the cheek and then sat down at the end of the conference table.

For a moment, the Reverend looked lost before finally walking out of the room.

"Okay, gang." Mrs. Walker clasped her hands together. "I think we should assign projects to everyone to make this more manageable. Hopefully then we won't have to have weekly meetings unless something important comes up."

"Makes sense," May said.

"Good. Barbara Ann, Peyton, and I would like to handle the food. Any objections?"

A chorus of *no*s sounded. Who would object to the best cooks preparing refreshments? Bebe hoped Mrs. Walker made more bread pudding.

"Great." Mrs. Walker beamed. "We need to decorate the town hall. May, are you still good with that?"

"Yes, ma'am."

"I can help with that," Sam offered.

"I don't mind either," Ryan said. He smiled at May, who glowed.

Good grief, Lord! What's gotten into her? Her friend had never behaved this way. And why would Jay's friend jump in to help? Wasn't he supposed to be watching over his patient?

"Thank you, Ryan. What about a theme?" Mrs. Walker looked around the table. "Last year we focused on the stars."

The focus had to be something that wouldn't cause the Reverend to have a stroke. "Since we're doing an angel tree beforehand, what about angels?" Jay asked. "Even though the gifts will be distributed before the ball, our decorations can reflect the theme. It'll be a reminder that we never know when we'll entertain the angels."

Bebe thought of the verse from Hebrews that said, *"Do not forget to entertain strangers, for by so doing some have unwittingly entertained angels."* Jay had a good point. She could picture the décor already.

"Great idea, son."

They ironed out more details, and Bebe relaxed as everything began to fall in place. This could work. They could celebrate Jesus and have fun. She wished the Reverend would loosen up. Sometimes he made it difficult to enjoy church. Peachwood Bay was small, and the only other church was a Catholic one. Since she wasn't Catholic, His House Fellowship was her only choice.

And she hated feeling that way about coming together to worship.

Trying to turn a lemon into lemonade was one of the reasons she volunteered. She'd hoped getting involved would make church attendance more bearable and less rigid-feeling.

"What about entertainment?"

Mrs. Walker's question yanked Bebe back into the discussion.

"I'll do it," she said.

"I'll help."

She glanced at Jay, her cheeks burning at their simultaneous offer.

"Oh, that would be just perfect, you two. Keep in mind it needs to be entertaining for adults *and* kids. 'Kay?"

Bebe nodded. More time with Jay? What had she gotten herself into?

Entertainment.

Jahleel had volunteered to help because he could do the job. But being thrown together with Bebe was probably more than he could handle. Something about being back in Peachwood Bay had him questioning past decisions. Hanging out with her yesterday reminded him how much he'd enjoyed their friendship . . . and her kisses. Could he plan the entertainment portion and keep his heart intact?

You have to! You're not staying in Peachwood.

He stared at the empty conference table. Ryan had left with May, probably going to dinner so they could moon over each other some more. The rest of the committee had left as soon as they received their assignments. Now he and Bebe sat trying to ignore the feelings flowing back and forth between them.

Or at least he was. His heart had been racing from the moment she walked into the church, green eyes glowing. "What should we do for fun?" he asked.

"Games?" Her gaze barely touched upon his face.

"What kind?"

"Um . . ."

"Surely you've been to a Christmas party before." Why was this so awkward when they'd had so much fun yesterday? Seeing her home come alive with the Christmas décor had loosened something inside him. He'd felt like he could breathe and remember why this season was so joyous. Now he felt awkward, thinking of how much more he'd have to fight from remembering their romantic past.

"Actually, it's been a while. Will preferred an upscale party with no games."

Ugh, he had no kind words to say about this guy. Jahleel wanted to make the entertainment work for everyone. "What do you like about parties?"

"The music."

"Write that down." He pointed toward her notebook. He

still couldn't believe Bebe Willabee—no, Gordon—was a schoolteacher. Then again, being a teacher wasn't so far removed from being a counselor. He was sure she was impacting students with that softness and inner glow that made kids gravitate toward her. She was like a gorgeous Mary Poppins.

"We should have a mix of songs. Include classical, contemporary, et cetera," Bebe suggested.

"Yes. Throw in some kid ones too. Like that hippo one."

She chuckled. "How do you know about that one?"

"The team does charity events for kids during the holiday season. I've heard quite a few hilarious ones."

"We should add something special. Magical, even?"

His father would *not* like that word, but he understood what she meant. "Mistletoe?"

Her cheeks flushed, and he bit back a grin.

"That's not what I meant."

"Okay, what, then?" He leaned back in his chair, lacing his fingers. Someway, somehow, he would sneak mistletoe into town hall. Maybe he could convince Ryan that it was a needed decoration.

"Reindeer?" She tilted her head in that way she did when concentrating.

But all Jay could concentrate on was the cascading hair that made him want to reach out and feel its softness. *Get it together, Walker. What did she just say?* "Wait, reindeer in Georgia?"

"Yes! There's a guy who owns a reindeer farm a county or two over. We could maybe do sleigh rides from the church to town hall. Charge a fee, which could cover the farmer's bill or go to another charity if we make enough."

"That's actually a fantastic idea, Bebe."

"I have them every now and again." A smug grin covered her adorable face.

"Ha." She was a riot. And gorgeous. So very gorgeous. He smothered a sigh. "What else?"

"I think we should have craft stations. The kids really liked those last year."

"Sounds good."

He listened, lobbing ideas back and forth as they ironed out more details. All the while he wanted to take her in his arms and ask if they could start over. Wasn't that the point of second chances? Sure, he'd asked for friendship, but why couldn't it lead to something more? It had their senior year. Couldn't that be an option again?

He sighed. *Lord, what do I do? There's no point wishing for something I can't have. I'm not staying here. I* can't *stay here.* There was nothing for him in Georgia. His father had made that abundantly clear. Not to mention that Jay would never step on the field as a football player again. Though that didn't mean his career in football was necessarily over. He could always make the transition to broadcasting, like so many others had. But he'd have to be in Texas for that, right? *Do you even want to be a broadcaster?*

The allure of a romantic relationship with Bebe called to him. Beckoned in the way she said his name.

"Jahleel?"

He blinked. Wait, she really *was* saying his name. "Sorry. I may have zoned out a bit."

"You think?" She chuckled. "Do you need some pain pills or something?"

"No, just a little distracted."

"By what?"

"You!" He groaned. "Sorry, didn't mean to shout."

A look of surprise widened her gaze. "How am I distracting you? I'm only taking notes."

"Bebe," he sighed. "You're you, and that has always distracted me. Well, once my hormones kicked in." He grinned, hoping to lighten the mood and erase his embarrassment.

"Jay, we can't go down that path again. We've already agreed friendship is best." She bit her lip, her brow furrowing with worry.

"Says who?" *You, you idiot.* Hadn't he just asked God to get his priorities right?

Her eyes widened. "We *both* did."

"I know, I know." He held up his hands. "But right now, I don't know if I want to."

"Are you even going to stay here in Peachwood Bay?"

He winced.

"I didn't think so." Her mouth flattened.

"Bebe, I don't know what my future holds, but I know I don't want to let go of you as easily as I did the last time."

"We can't always have what we want." She looked away, lost in thought.

Was she thinking of her ex? Was that why she was so hesitant to give him a chance? Or was it worse . . . was she still in love with what's-his-face? Jay paused for a moment, searching for the right words. He took a breath.

"If the other one is willing to take a chance, then I think we can have what we want."

Her lips pursed. "Then I guess I'm not willing." She grabbed her notebook and stuffed it into her humongous tote bag. "I'll get started on these. Bye, Jay."

"Bebe . . ."

She continued walking until he could no longer hear her footfalls. What could he do to get her to stop saying good-bye?

Chapter
EIGHT

"Come on, Mama." Hope pulled Bebe through the crowd, trying to get a good spot to watch the Peachwood Bay Christmas Parade.

The thing about the parade that Bebe loved the most was that it was a waterway event. Those who owned boats went all out in decorating their ships with Christmas lights or even adding inflatables.

"Can we get some hot chocolate?" Hope asked. She pointed to a stand that had a few people in line.

"Of course. Is it even the boat parade without hot chocolate to keep us warm?" Bebe smiled into her daughter's face.

"Not at all," a deep voice said behind them.

Bebe whirled around and met Jay's happy face. His lips curved in a half smile that could have been a smirk or just him trying to be cute. *Cute, definitely cute.*

"Hey, I didn't expect to see you here."

His brows rose. "You did say I should bring Ryan to the parade." He pointed to his friend.

She glanced at the man beside Jay. She'd almost—*almost*—missed his presence. "Yep. I did." She swallowed. "You should try the hot chocolate. It's the best." Thank goodness the darkness hid her blush. She felt so foolish right now.

"You still sticking peppermint sticks in your hot chocolate, Bebe?" Jay's eyes seemed to dance with merriment.

Was he truly happy recalling that, or was it the hope of Christmas that made her heart flutter since he remembered such a minor detail?

"She does!" Hope chimed in. "I like it too. Do you?"

"I sure do." Jay gave her a wink.

"Then your friend has to get a peppermint stick too," Hope said.

"Sounds good to me!" Ryan said, smiling.

Somehow, Bebe found herself next to Jay as they got in line for hot chocolate. She couldn't help but recall his plea to be more than friends. Now she felt awkward. Life would be so much easier moving forward as friends. She wouldn't have to wonder if he was making a play for her heart since he couldn't play on the field. She didn't want to be second choice to a sport or even a fallback plan since he was sidelined right now. Only that seemed like too much word vomit to spew out in public when they were here for Christmas cheer.

"What else is the same about you, Bebe Willabee?" Jay's smooth tenor sent goose bumps of awareness up her arms.

"I haven't changed much," she responded.

He studied her. "I'm sure that's true but also not. We all change in some ways. I look forward to learning the current Bebe."

Her throat constricted. Did that mean he'd be here long enough to learn more about her current quirks, her likes and dislikes? Somehow, she couldn't imagine Jay in Peachwood long-term.

"Jay . . ."

"Hmm?"

"What are you hoping to prove? If you want to be my friend

and catch up and be present now, fine. We can be friends. We spent a childhood doing so." She paused, gathering courage to defend her heart. "But if it's something more you're looking for, then I would caution you to stop right here."

"Why?"

She stepped forward, noticing the gap between them and the people in front of them. "Because I'm not the same girl you liked in high school. I'm a mom, and I just can't jump into a relationship, especially one that has no future."

He stared at her, but his face remained impassive. Had she hurt his feelings, or was he merely thinking over her words?

"How do you know we have no future?"

"I mean, it's pretty obvious. I live in Peachwood, and you'll return to Texas after the holidays." She shrugged. "That's not a recipe for a relationship."

"People do long-distance and get stronger for it."

"But in the end, someone always moves."

"I just think you shouldn't discount us because of our mailing addresses. You're not God, Bebe. You can't see the future."

Her mouth dropped. She wanted to argue, but he had a point.

"Do you have to know the end before you can start at the beginning?" he asked.

"No," she mumbled.

He smirked. "Sure, you don't. But that's okay." He motioned her forward. "Let me pay for y'all's hot chocolate. While you're sipping your drink, think about us. We're good as friends, but you and I both know we're much better in a romantic relationship."

Bebe could argue, but Hope turned around at that moment and spoke. "They have marshmallows, Mama. Can I have those in my drink too?"

"Of course."

They got their drinks, and Bebe thanked Jay.

"Do you want to sit with us?" Hope asked.

Jay smiled softly at her. "Thank you for the invitation, but Ryan is saving a spot for us. I hope you enjoy the parade."

"You too, Mr. Walker."

Bebe let Hope guide her to a good spot along the harbor. Soon, Peachwood Bay's Santa would ring his sleigh bells, and the boats would begin to float down the canal, showcasing their decorations. There would be a town vote on the best boat décor, and the owner would get a check from the mayor. It was usually a couple of hundred dollars, certainly not the kind of check Jahleel got for playing football, but one that meant the world to the townspeople during the holiday season.

Bebe sat on a concrete bench and scooted Hope close to her. "Warm?"

"Yes."

"Remember to blow on your hot chocolate." Usually, the vendor made kids' cups less hot than the adults' so they wouldn't burn their mouths. Still, Bebe couldn't keep from cautioning her daughter.

"I will, Mama."

Just then, sleigh bells rang. The crowd gasped as a "Ho, ho, ho" reverberated through the crowd.

Hope stood, attempting to peek around the crowd.

"Give him a sec, Hope. You know his boat will sail right past us."

"I know, but I want to see him now. Why couldn't we sit at the beginning of the parade?"

Because that was where she and Jay had always sat. Bebe blinked. Was that right? Had her subconscious been keeping her from memories of Jay all this time? She gulped. What did it say that being back in Peachwood Bay constantly reminded her of her first love? And was Jay right, insinuating that they could be great together?

No, that's not the plan. You stay friends, and when he leaves for Texas, you might *keep in touch.* Though she wouldn't bank on that. She'd been foolish to believe that before. No way she wanted to make the same mistakes once more.

Bebe pushed the thoughts aside and watched her daughter as glee covered her face when the Santa's sleigh–themed boat floated right in front of them. Bebe grabbed her cell and took a picture of Hope, then the boat, before pocketing the phone.

She wanted to remember this time with her daughter. With Will being an absent parent, Bebe was more cognizant of how fast time went and how important it was to show up.

Jay wants to show up.

She stuffed down a scoff. Jahleel had caught the love of Christmas and nostalgia wrapped in one. She couldn't trust his feelings were real because she'd done that before and had the burn marks to prove it wasn't what she'd hoped.

Never again.

But another part of her heart said, *Never say never.*

⸻

"You've got it bad," Ryan said.

Jahleel snorted. "I'm not the one who turns beet red and can't take my eyes off a certain woman whose name is the same as a month of the year."

"May's awesome, but that's beside the point. We're talking about you and Bebe. She's the one, right?"

"The one what?" Jay asked just to hear what Ryan would say.

"The one who got away? You have that lovesick longing expression on your face."

Jay shook his head. "More like I'm the idiot who let her get away and now I'd like another chance."

Ryan blew out a breath. "I don't know what to tell you, bro." He stopped, staring out at the canal as the Santa sleigh sailed by. Then he turned to Jahleel. "What's the story? Is she the woman you dated in high school?"

Jay nodded.

"Ohhh," Ryan drew out. "Yeah, I have no tips except maybe grovel. You left her without a backward glance. That had to have stung."

"And now she's divorced, so kind of a double whammy, right?"

Ryan shook his head. "You need a Christmas miracle to get back in her good graces."

"She said we could be friends."

"I guess the friend zone is the only end zone you'll be getting in this season."

Ouch. Jahleel rubbed his chest to take away the sting from the imaginary dart Ryan threw his way.

"Too soon?" Ryan asked quietly.

"You're not wrong."

"Still, that was probably a little insensitive."

Jay sighed and leaned back in the lawn chair Ryan had set up. "Forgetting about my bum leg for a moment, do you honestly think it'll take a Christmas miracle to win Bebe back?"

"Without a doubt. You probably hurt her in ways you'll never understand by severing ties. Then her husband did the same—at least, I'm assuming."

"You assume right." Jahleel's jaw clenched just thinking about that man.

"Then you waltz back into town wanting her back? How does she know it's not because you have no other opportunities before you?" Ryan asked.

"Man, are you playing devil's advocate?"

"Nah, just trying to get you to see the mountain you're facing."

Jay nodded slowly. "So you're saying I'm facing Super Bowl champs, and I'm the underdog?"

"Worse, you're the team no one likes and hopes to see fail."

He winced. "I can't be that bad, can I?" But as soon as the

words left his mouth, he realized it was true. He was like the Patriots going to the Super Bowl. Everyone loved to cheer for the other team, and the only ones rooting for a Pats win were the New England states.

"How can I show her I'm not a bad man? That my intentions are serious?" Because the more he thought about Bebe, the more he wanted a second chance.

He didn't know the future, didn't know what would happen to them beyond today, but that didn't scare him. If anything, Jahleel wanted to lean on God's wisdom and pray that He had a second chance lined up for them. One that would go the distance and overcome any potential conflict.

"Start by showing up. Invite her out to do something fun. Show her you're listening to her and to God's leading. Show her you're not the Jahleel of the past who hurt her but that you've matured in the areas you needed growth."

"Man, how did you get so wise?"

"You're not the first person to hurt a woman's heart, and you won't be the last."

They quieted as boat after boat sailed by. There was a boat that looked like it had been transformed into a floating gingerbread house, one with a snowman family on it, and one with reindeer. Ryan enjoyed himself, so Jay felt he'd done well in showing a little bit of Peachwood Bay to his friend. Even though he was paying the physical therapist's rate, he was fully aware Ryan didn't have to fly out here just to help him.

Jay looked at Ryan. "Now that we're done talking about me, what's going on with you and May?"

Ryan's face turned red. "Not much to tell right now."

"That's not what your face is saying."

Ryan huffed out a strained laugh. "I like her." He shrugged. "It's as simple as that."

"But you don't live here, and she doesn't live in Tennessee."

"We're not worried about distance. Right now, we just want to see how much we like each other, then go from there."

Was it that easy? Then again, they had no shared history like he and Bebe did. "You take her out yet?"

"We're going out tomorrow night. She's with her folks today, otherwise she would've come with us to the parade."

Jay couldn't say much because part of him was jealous. Ryan had it easy. He liked May, asked her out, and she was willing. As simple as that. But that wasn't his path. Jahleel's was filled with boulders, lava, and other treacherous obstacles. Yet he knew in his heart that Bebe was worth it.

It was time to work out a game plan to win Bebe Gordon's heart.

Chapter
NINE

The line for donuts ended in the vestibule a corridor away from the conference room where they were displayed. All Bebe wanted to do was go home, curl up in front of the TV, and watch the Falcons play. Instead, she waited in line for a donut with Hope. Her girl lived for the powdered ones every Sunday. Bebe preferred the glazed donuts, which would most likely be gone by the time they made it to the front of the line.

The hairs on the back of her neck rose to attention as the smell of lemon and a woody undertone enveloped her. The urge to lean back into Jay's arms overwhelmed her. Why did he keep showing up wherever she was?

Straightening her shoulders, Bebe turned slightly. "What are you doing standing up?" She grimaced inwardly at her tone. That hadn't been what she wanted to say or the tone she wanted to use.

"I want a donut." He gave her a boyish smile.

Why did her pulse have to flutter?

"Mr. Walker, you should rest." Hope looked at him, her brow furrowed.

Bebe stifled a chuckle.

"Then how can I get a donut?" he asked.

"I'll get you one." Hope rolled her eyes. "Don't you know when you're supposed to ask for help? Grown-ups," she mumbled.

Jay's face lit with laughter, the crinkles around his eyes joining in the joke. "I suppose that means I should sit back down?"

"Yes, sir." Hope dipped her head, hands folded primly in front of her. "We'll find you and bring you a donut."

"Thank you." He turned to Bebe, leaning close. "See you soon, Bebe Gordon."

An ominous flush went down her spine. At least, she told herself it was ominous. She refused to entertain anything further with this man. He would go back to Texas and live the rest of his life there, and she would stay in Peachwood Bay.

Why?

Bebe blinked. What kind of question was that?

But then, why *did* she want to stay in this town? Coming back home after her divorce had been a temporary Plan B, not any fulfillment of a lifelong dream. But the only time Texas had ever been on her radar was when Jay got accepted to UT. She'd thought about transferring after a semester to be with him, since she'd already been accepted to Georgia Tech. Except Jay had ended their relationship without a backward glance. Once again, her dreams had gone out the window.

Don't plan your life around a man again, Bebe.

But she couldn't help but remember his words from the other night. *"Honestly, I don't know what my future holds, but I know I don't want to let go of you as easily as I did the last time."*

Then he'd shown up to the boat parade and now behind her in the donut line. Was he being serious about his intentions or merely bored? Could they actually have a future this time?

"You're not God, Bebe. You can't see the future."

Ugh she did *not* want to hear Jay's voice in her head. Besides, men like him did *not* stick around. They threw money at the situation and abdicated their responsibility. Jay hadn't stepped foot in their hometown in over eight years. *Eight years!* That had to be a sign that this reaction to him was simply hormonal. Who wouldn't feel some sort of spark at seeing their first love again, right?

"Hey, Bebe."

She smiled at May, giving her a hug. "Hey, May. I didn't see you in service." They always sat together.

"Sorry, girl. I sat with Ryan."

"Ryan?"

"You know, Jay's physical therapist?"

"Wow. You guys seem awfully . . ." What? Chummy? Glued at the hip? Cliché after cliché danced through Bebe's mind.

"Smitten." A soft smile graced May's face.

"Don't you think it's too fast? You just met." Something that felt very much like—*jealousy?*—churned in Bebe's stomach.

"Calm down, girl. No one's declaring their undying devotion any time soon. We're just enjoying a little flirting and the getting-to-know-you period. You know"—she nudged Bebe's hip—"what you used to do when you dated."

Bebe snorted. "Dating, right."

"Don't let Will turn you all cynical," May whispered as she slipped an arm around Bebe's shoulders.

Bebe glanced at her daughter, then continued in a whisper. "I'm not. I'm realistic."

"Says every cynic."

"I'm just saying, when you move too fast, you get burned." Her mind flitted to Jay, then Will. Each time, she'd placed her plans for their future above reality. And crashed back down *painfully* when life happened.

"Sometimes, Bebe, it seems fast to those who don't know God's plan."

Her eye twitched. "Are you saying you think God wants the two of you to be together?"

"He's not saying no. And believe me, I ask about every potential man. This is the first time I have warm fuzzies." May got a faraway look in her eyes.

Bebe wrapped her arms around her waist, glanced at Hope, then May, and lowered her voice further. "I wish I had done that with Will."

"It's not too late."

"Will's already remarried." Besides, she wanted nothing to do with him. He broke their covenant the moment he slept with Angie.

"Not with *him*." May made a sound of disgust. "I'm talking about Jay. Come on, think about it. The man just happens to blow out a knee within driving distance of his hometown? Where you live because you returned three years ago? Maybe your timing is finally right now."

Bebe's stomach did a funny flip. Would God really use Jahleel's knee injury to bring them together? Could May be onto something?

"Think about us. We're good as friends, but you and I both know we're much better in a romantic relationship."

"Think about it, Bebe. Okay?"

First Jay and now May. All Bebe could do was nod, too stunned to speak. *Lord, what do I do? You wouldn't really put us back together, would You? I mean, isn't there too much hurt, too much pain, a lack of trust, even?* She bit her lip, subconsciously taking the next steps to propel her through the donut line. *I'm sorry I never asked if Will was for me, Lord. I pray that You would bless me with wisdom. Help me to know if Jay's for me or if this is some crazy Christmas magic–induced brain haze. In Jesus's name, amen.*

Hope clapped her hands with delight. They were next in line. Her daughter reached for two plates, a glazed and powdered donut plate.

"Just one, Hope dear. We have to make sure everyone gets a plate," Ms. Barbara Ann stated.

"I'm getting one for Mr. Walker since he can't walk so good."

"Aren't you just a peach." Barbara Ann beamed at Hope, then turned to Bebe. "You're doing a fine job, Mama."

"Thank you." *It's all You, Lord.* She thanked Him for her beautiful little girl. Bebe rubbed Hope's shoulder in praise.

As they headed toward Jay, Bebe braced herself. She had no idea when God would answer her prayer and bless her with wisdom. Until then, she'd continue to guard her heart and ensure Jahleel Walker wouldn't catch it, only to fumble and leave her bruised and hurting.

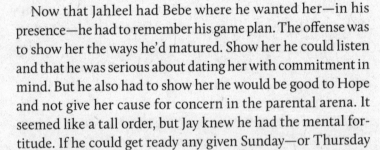

Now that Jahleel had Bebe where he wanted her—in his presence—he had to remember his game plan. The offense was to show her the ways he'd matured. Show her he could listen and that he was serious about dating her with commitment in mind. But he also had to show her he would be good to Hope and not give her cause for concern in the parental arena. It seemed like a tall order, but Jay knew he had the mental fortitude. If he could get ready any given Sunday—or Thursday or Monday night, or playoff Saturday—prepared to be tackled as he headed for the end zone, then he could handle whatever Bebe threw his way. His skill as a wide receiver was top-notch. Instead of catching a football, he wanted to catch her heart.

Bebe Gordon was all warmth and joy. Her overall personality still tugged at him like it had in high school. Somehow he felt grounded when he was around her. She was the only woman who brought out this side in him. Not only that, but time with the Lord had given Jahleel the mindset that God would okay their dating life *and* future.

Would she shoot him down if he asked her on a date right now?

Never know unless you ask.

And therein lay the crux. It terrified him to think of her rejection, which meant he also felt immense guilt for rejecting her in the past. Ryan was right. Jay needed a Hail Mary or, in this case, a Christmas miracle.

"Do you like your donut, Mr. Walker?"

He looked at Hope. The same green eyes as her mother shone in her warm brown face. Her hair had been parted down the middle and gathered into two curly pigtails. She was adorable. "It's perfect. Thanks, Hope."

"You're welcome!" She beamed at him.

Yep, adorable. "How's yours?" He pointed to her plate.

"Great! Powdered ones are my fav," she said around a mouthful.

"Hope," Bebe scolded.

Her daughter gave a sheepish smile, cheeks puffed up like a chipmunk. He chuckled, staring at Bebe inconspicuously out of the corner of his eye. Then he glanced toward Ryan and May, who were grinning from ear-to-ear. Ryan had the right idea. Just lay it all out. No games. No pretenses. Just be himself.

You got this, Walker.

"Bebe . . ."

"Yes?" She looked up at him.

Breathe, Walker. "Would you go out with me?"

She blinked. Her mouth parted.

He gulped, hating the silence that lengthened between them. "Bebe?"

"Sure." The look on her face was hesitant, but her voice was certain.

A whoosh of air left his lungs. She'd said yes. *Yes!* He couldn't have contained his grin if he tried. "Great."

"It can be a working date. We'll check out the reindeer." She grinned and took the last bite of her donut.

His shoulders dropped. A working date? *Really?* Then again, if that made her more comfortable, he would agree to it. "Deal." He offered his hand, bracing for . . . what, he wasn't sure.

She glanced down and carefully placed her hand in his. He squeezed it lightly, then let go despite the longing to hold on.

"What's a date?" Hope stared up at him quizzically.

Oops. He'd forgotten all about her for a moment. *Smooth move, Walker.*

"A date is when two people go somewhere together to have fun," Bebe explained.

"Oh. Then we go on dates all the time, Mama."

He chuckled. "That's because she's fun to be around, isn't she?"

"The best." Hope's smile turned into a frown. "I wish my dad would take me on a date. He's always too busy." She sighed. "Or maybe he doesn't think I'm any fun." Her bottom lip quivered.

If he ever met Bebe's ex-husband he'd . . . Jahleel released a deep breath. "Some grown-ups forget to have fun. It doesn't mean that you're not fun. It's their problem, not yours, 'kay?"

Hope smiled with relief.

Bebe flashed him a look of gratitude. He nodded, too upset to say anything else. What made a man think he could have a child and just be done, never showing up when needed? Despite the issues he had with his own father, Obadiah Walker had always been there. Granted, he rained judgment every opportunity he could get, but his presence had never been lacking. It was one of the reasons Jahleel had applied to an out-of-state school. He needed to breathe. Become his own man without the self-righteous judgment of his father weighing him down.

Seeing Hope, part of him felt guilty for not seeing the blessing of a two-parent home.

"Would you go out on a date with me, Mr. Walker? Or could you come to one of my flag football games?" Hope peered up at him.

"You play flag football?" He glanced between her and Bebe, who nodded.

"Yep. I'm one of the running backs, and then I switch and get to play safety."

"That's awesome, Hope. I'd love to come."

She threw her arms around him, squeezing with all her seven-year-old might. "Great! My game is next Saturday."

"I'll be there."

Hope turned and then squealed. She looked at Bebe. "I see Jenny. Can I go say hi?"

"Of course."

She took off running.

"Walk!" Bebe called after her.

Hope speed-walked the rest of the way.

Jahleel let loose a laugh. "That girl's a pistol."

"Yes, she is."

"And you love her for it."

Bebe's grin widened. "It's like watching your heart beat. I would do anything for her."

"You're a great mom."

"Thank you." She met his gaze. "And thank you for what you said to her. She doesn't always show her hurt so easily. Sometimes I forget she's only seven."

"She probably wants to be tough like you." Bebe had taken many hits in life and still exuded a peace and strength that baffled him. But it also made him want the same thing for his life. Could he deal with his father just as peacefully?

"Ha. I'm a cream puff."

"Nah, more like a prickly pear." He winked.

"Way to charm a girl, Jahleel."

He shivered. She was the only person who made his whole

name sound so melodic. He actually preferred it when she used his full name, although he'd never admit it aloud. "I have my moments."

A laugh burst free from her lips, her hair curtaining her face. She tucked it back behind her ear. "You've got jokes, for sure."

"Anything to see you smile." Because the transformation on her face was breathtaking. Light shined forth brighter than any Christmas lights. He couldn't look away if he wanted to. And he totally didn't.

A blush stained Bebe's cheeks, and she fiddled with her napkin and empty plate.

"When's the last time you had a good laugh, Bebe?"

"Hope makes me laugh."

"That I can believe, but I mean with adults. When you're not so worried about presenting a good front."

"I . . ." She shrugged. "Who knows, Jay. Life's been rough these past three years. Longer, really."

"Well, it's a good thing we're going to have fun on our date."

"Oh, really?"

"Yes, ma'am. Be prepared." He winked while his mind raced forward.

What could he do to ensure it was the best date she'd ever had? Because Bebe Gordon deserved the best.

Chapter
TEN

Bebe reached for her cell as she shifted the grocery bags in her hand. "Hello?"

"Hey, baby girl. How are you?"

"Hi, Dad." Her cheeks pushed upward. She loved talking with her father. "I'm just walking in the door with the groceries. Give me a sec."

"Sure."

"I'll take it, Mama."

"Thanks, Hope."

Hope pressed the phone to her ear. "Hi, Grandpa." The rest of the conversation became muted as Bebe headed for the kitchen counter.

It never failed—whenever she needed to put groceries away, someone always called. Not that she minded terribly. It helped the mundane task pass quickly. Except Hope had her phone, and she was forced to do the task alone. After stowing the last item in the fridge, Bebe beckoned to her daughter.

"Mama's ready to talk now, Grandpa." Hope looked away. "Love you too." She handed Bebe the phone. "May I watch TV?"

"Sure, pumpkin." She took her earring out of her right ear and slid the phone against it. "I'm back, Dad."

"Grocery shopping, huh?"

"Yes. You know me. I can never seem to make it a full week."

His deep belly laugh filtered through the phone. "Ain't that the truth. But you have enough to make cookies, don't you?"

Her cheeks heated as she remembered making sugar cookies with Jay. The football-shaped treats had been delicious, as had the Christmas tree–shaped one she'd grabbed before heading to the store.

"I hit it on the nail, didn't I?" He chuckled.

"Sure did."

"How are my girls doing?"

"Good. School goes on break soon. Oh, and the church is having a Christmas ball on Christmas Eve at the town hall."

"Really? Obadiah approved that?"

Bebe held in her amusement. "I think Mrs. Walker persuaded him. Plus, it helped that Jahleel offered to pay all expenses."

"Jay's still in town? That knee really sidelined him, huh?"

"Yeah." She sighed. Jay hadn't mentioned anything further about his career, but last Sunday he was placed on the injured reserve list. That had to gnaw at him.

"How you doin', seeing him again after all these years?"

Trust her dad to be concerned. The thought warmed her. "He asked me out."

"Oh, re-al-ly?" Her dad drawled. "I think this is where I get off the phone and hand it over to your mother."

"Bye, Dad," she chuckled.

"Bye, baby girl. See you soon."

"I will?"

"Hank," her mother shouted in the background. "Way to let the surprise out."

"Oops," he whispered. "Say a prayer for me, Bebe. She's got a hand on her hip."

She loved her parents. They never stayed mad at each other for too long. Probably because her dad cracked a joke and earned a *you're forgiven* smile from her mother.

"Bebe, dear, don't pay your father any mind."

"So you aren't coming to visit?"

A groan greeted her ears. "Of course we're coming. It was *supposed* to be a surprise. Now I'll just have to think of another way to surprise you."

"Come to the Christmas ball."

"Who's having a ball?"

"The church. On Christmas Eve." Giddiness filled her. The thought of celebrating with the Peachwood Bay community and wearing a fancy dress had her counting down the days. This was the best idea ever, and she prayed Reverend Walker would love it enough for it to become a tradition.

"Is this where the date comes in?"

"Sort of. I'm working on the entertainment for the ball with Jahleel. We're going out this Friday. Kind of a work date." *Because I turned it into one.* Knowing Jay, that wouldn't stop him from making his real intentions known.

"How long is he back in town for?"

"Until he's healed, I imagine." Her stomach dipped. She needed that reminder that he lived in Texas and she was in Georgia. Once again, the thought of something long-term seemed out of reach.

"So you're not sure of the exact time frame?" Her mother's voice sounded . . . irritated?

"No, Mama."

"Then do you think it's wise to go out with him? Don't you remember—"

"I remember, Mama." She rubbed her forehead. "We're just going to look at reindeer."

"Bebe, I don't have a problem with you dating him. I just want to make sure you're healed from the last time. To make sure you've forgiven him, because in order to not fall apart at his leaving again, you need to come to terms with everything in the past."

Did she? Was there some requirement that you had to know what you were doing before you did it? That was how she'd been approaching this whole situation with Jay. If she didn't know there was a happy-ever-after waiting for her, Bebe didn't want to go after the dream.

And maybe that was something she needed to work on with the Lord. Surely God didn't want her to live like that, scared of pain and sorrow. He'd promised to be with her no matter what and had promised that trials would come. So how did Bebe guard her heart but live an abundant life at the same time? Were the two contrary?

"All right, Mama."

"Good. Now make sure you have fun. I can't remember the last time you did so."

Did everyone think of her as a fuddy-duddy? "I will." She kept the long-suffering sigh inside. No need to incur her mother's lecture on being disrespectful.

"Good. Then my job here is done. Put my grandbaby on the phone."

Bebe called for Hope and handed her the cell. Sitting on a barstool, she sighed. Part of her was looking forward to her outing with Jay. They'd go look at some reindeer, hopefully secure them for the ball, and enjoy each other's company in the process. And all the while, thoughts of Jahleel returning to Texas would be stuffed out of reach. She didn't want to walk that path again. It was too reminiscent of her high school days.

Maybe her mama was right. She just needed to let it go, give it to God, and press forward. But could she? *Lord, please help me forgive the past and heal so I can enjoy the present.*

She watched as Hope giggled and chatted happily with her grandmother. If something did develop between her and Jay, would moving to Texas be a given? Could she take Hope away from all she knew? Peachwood Bay was the only home her little girl remembered. And was she absolutely out of her mind to even think of moving to another state before going on a date with the man? *You're getting ahead of yourself. Slow down.*

"Yes," she whispered. "Don't fall first and fast. That's where failure is. Just take it one day at a time."

Just because Jay flirted with a boyish grin or offered to go to Hope's football game didn't mean Bebe had to fall at his feet. She'd save the swooning for her mental gymnastics.

A groan tore from her lips, and she dropped her head onto the kitchen counter. Going to Hope's football game was a biggie.

***

He was going to need a job.

Jahleel leaned against his forearms as they rested on the kitchen table. "What am I going to do, Ryan?"

The Desperados' general manager had informed his agent that they were not renegotiating his contract. His agent had immediately passed on the message. Jahleel could either retire or become a free agent at the end of his contract. Since Ryan had already snuffed out Jay's chances of playing again, being a free agent obviously wasn't an option. His therapy was progressing well, but at this point, Jay wasn't even sure he should push himself to try to prove Ryan's diagnosis wrong. If the Desperados weren't going to re-sign him and essentially felt his career was over, Jahleel should simply aim for walking without a limp. But to actually say he'd retire . . .

"What do you want to do?" His friend stretched his feet out in front of him. "You have a business degree and years of experience in the NFL. Looks like you have two pathways."

"I'm not sure I want to switch to broadcasting or to the analysis side of the NFL. Talking about it isn't the same as playing." Jahleel shifted his leg, noting the odd way his knee felt without his brace. Ryan had him going through range-of-motion exercises, and the relief of not being constrained kept him from focusing on the pain of the movements. "I have no idea what I'd even do with my business degree."

"Why did you get it?"

Good question. "Actually, I wanted to own my own business." He sat back. How had he forgotten that?

"Selling what?"

"Sports memorabilia." His grin stretched wide. He was in a perfect position to start. But where?

"That's a great idea. Except where would you open it? You are thinking brick-and-mortar versus online, right?"

"I was just wondering which direction to go." Jay couldn't imagine staying in Peachwood Bay, even if he somehow managed to get on good terms with his father. The town was just too small for a sports memorabilia store to actually rake in income.

But if he had an online store, he could potentially store items in an office space in his home or rent out a storage unit.

Ryan rubbed his beard, his gaze direct. "So what's happening with you and Bebe?"

"We're going out on Friday." He couldn't stop the grin on his face. "She wants it to be a working date. Only I kind of made some other arrangements that make it a *date* date." She was going to love it . . . he hoped. The Bebe he knew in the past would love his plans. He hoped it was also the right move for the Bebe of now.

"Does that mean Peachwood Bay is a prospect?" Ryan raised a brow.

"I don't know if there's a market for something like that here. Atlanta, yes. But people down here like seafood, boats, and football. Probably in that order too."

"Yeah, but football and the South go hand in hand. I'm sure people own plenty of sports memorabilia down here. Don't overlook the potential."

Was he? He'd never thought much of his hometown. Sure, he loved the water and the views the Atlantic had to offer. Even enjoyed the Spanish moss that hung from the oak trees. Then again, he always pictured Bebe leaning against one, her hair cascading over her shoulders, green eyes bright with laughter. No, when he thought of Peachwood Bay, Bebe remained front and center. Not the locale or things to do.

But could he go back to Texas without her? Maybe if he could leave with a promise, it wouldn't be so bad. After all, long-distance relationships could work. All he needed was a promise they could work toward something more. Something involving a ring and green-eyed children.

"Walker!"

His head jerked toward Ryan. "Sorry, what?"

"I was asking what you had planned," Ryan laughed. "But apparently you were living it out."

"Yeah, I kind of zoned out." He rubbed the back of his neck. "We're going to a reindeer farm, so I made a date close by."

"A reindeer farm in Georgia?" Ryan's brow furrowed.

"Yep. We want them for the ball. Bebe thought it would be great to have sleigh rides from the church to the town hall."

"That is pretty ingenious."

"That's my girl." At least in his mind. Now to make his dreams reality.

Ryan stood, clapping a hand on his shoulder. "I'll be praying God guides you."

"Thanks, man." He slowly rose to his feet, thankful for the aid of a crutch. "What about you and May?"

"That's easier. The difference between Tennessee and Georgia isn't so vast. Plus, we're still taking it one day at a time."

But the grin on his face told Jahleel they were moving in the right direction.

"True." Should he consider moving back to Georgia? Enjoy a slower pace of life with Bebe and Hope?

"Remember, brace off at home. Let your knee remember its job. Brace on outside the house. And do *not* forget to do your exercises."

"Got it, O'Neal. Get on out of here."

"Don't have to tell me twice." Ryan grinned and headed for the front door. "I'll see myself out."

As he reached the front door, it opened, and in walked Jahleel's father.

Great.

He'd lost count what round they were in. Jahleel had stopped holding his tongue. If he wasn't careful, a repeat of his college graduation was bound to happen. And he wasn't quite ready to head back to Texas. He planned to stay at least through Christmas Day.

"Have a good day, Reverend." Ryan tossed a wave over his shoulder.

"So spoiled you have to get house visits." His father grunted, placing his house keys on the hook by the door. "I never would have infringed on a friend like that in my day."

"You had friends?" Jay turned away to regain his composure. *Smart-aleck comments won't help the situation.*

"Plenty. Ones I didn't desert, and ones who didn't desert me."

Jahleel's head shot up, and his eyes locked onto those of Obadiah Walker. "Is that what you think? That I abandoned you? No, sir. You did that a long time ago."

"'Honor your father and your mother, that your days may be long upon the land which the Lord your God is giving you.'"

"'Fathers, do not provoke your children, lest they become discouraged,'" he shot back.

His father's jaw clenched, bulging near his ears.

"All my life, all I ever wanted was your approval," Jahleel said. "A kind word. But no, you couldn't give an inch of compassion where I was concerned. I'm not even sure if you give your congregants the mercy they need. What's it like, seeing sin in every corner and ignoring it in your own life?"

"You will not speak to me in that manner."

"That's just fine because I have nothing more to say." Jahleel headed for his bedroom. His scalp prickled. His muscles twitched from the death grip he had on his crutch.

"Don't walk away from me when I'm talking to you, boy."

Jahleel paused, head down. "I'm not a child." He lifted his head and stared right back at his father. "I'm a man who deserves just as much respect as you demand. And right now, I need to leave before I say something I'll regret."

And with that, he continued toward his sanctuary.

Chapter
ELEVEN

Bebe's frame shook lightly as her leg jiggled up and down. Its steady rhythm didn't penetrate the mental haze as she stared at the clock. Knowing mobility was an issue, she'd offered to pick Jay up to go to the reindeer farm, only he insisted on doing things the *right* way. Which meant she'd been dressed and ready to go half an hour ago, as if this outing was a true date and didn't bear the *work* moniker she'd attempted to force on it. Would they have fun today? And how could she make it fifteen more minutes before their *work date* began without contemplating what the future could possibly look like between them?

Lord, why does my mind automatically go to the future? You tell me not to worry about tomorrow, and I don't want to. I want to rest in today and be present in the moment. Please help my thoughts focus on the now instead of the what-if.

She popped off the couch and headed into the kitchen. A drink of water might steady her nerves. The filtered water sloshed as she poured it into a mason jar. The first sip brought relief to the intense dryness in her throat. The second sip reminded her she'd been down this road before. Dating Jahleel wasn't anything new.

Except now you have a child. Who had been all too happy to go to Rosa's to play with her daughter.

Bebe placed the glass against her forehead, reveling in the coolness. The cowl neck sweater she'd paired with her dark-wash jeans made her uncomfortably warm. Or it could be the troop of rabbits stomping their feet in her stomach.

The doorbell pealed, echoing in her quiet home. She gasped. Her mason jar dropped into the sink, rolling around. *Get a grip. It's Jay. It's not the first time you've been alone with him.* She slid her hands down her pant legs, then headed for the door. *Don't be nervous. Don't be nervous.*

Pasting a pleasant expression on her face, Bebe opened the door. Her heart dropped to her knees as Jay held out a bouquet of white roses—her favorite flowers.

"You remembered?" she breathed.

His lips quirked into a crooked grin. "I did."

"They're gorgeous." She took them, inhaling their rich fragrance. He had given her white roses on prom night as well. She shoved those memories way. "Thank you."

"You're welcome." He nodded toward her kitchen. "Why don't you put those in some water so we can be on our way."

"Right." She gave a shaky grin, then turned away. *Oh my goodness*, she mouthed to herself.

Jay looked gorgeous, wearing a red leather jacket that should've been flashy but came across as confident and made her want to snuggle into the warmth of his arms. A black knit beanie covered his head and somehow made him even more handsome. In the kitchen, she blew air up across her face, hoping to cool her hot cheeks. What was it about him that made her lightheaded? Breathless? And desperately in need of a show of affection?

Every time she was around Jahleel Walker, Bebe forgot

exactly why she should be protesting a relationship between them. *Maybe that means stop protesting.*

She gulped as she made her way back to him. He held out her black peacoat, and that was when she noticed the cane.

"Wait. Where are your crutches?" Wasn't he supposed to be on them for another two weeks?

"Ryan thinks the cane is fine as long as I wear my brace, just for tonight."

"That's good, right?"

He nodded.

Bebe murmured her thanks as Jay slipped on her jacket. The scent of lemon and wood wrapped around her.

"You're welcome."

She felt the touch of his breath against her neck, and the hairs on her arms shot up. She faced him, then took a step back.

He dipped his head slightly and gestured for her to head outside with his hand. "Your chariot awaits, milady."

A chuckle escaped at his awful accent, which quickly morphed into a gasp. "A limo?"

A long white car waited at the end of her driveway. A man in a black suit stood next to the vehicle, hands clasped in front of him.

"I figured since I couldn't afford one in high school, I'd make up for that now," Jahleel said.

Unease skittered down her spine. "You don't have to throw your money around." That was the first thing Will would do. *They're not the same. Stop comparing.* She bit back a sigh.

"I know." His brow furrowed. "This is called making a good impression. Just because you want it to be a working date doesn't mean I'll stick entirely to those parameters."

Bebe nodded. He wasn't Will. Just the boy who left her without a word. *When are you going to forgive him for making a difficult decision?* Football was always Jay's dream, and maybe that was the problem. She feared she'd never measure up to the sport that made him a star.

"What's going on in that brain of yours?" he asked.

"I'm . . ." She licked her lips. "I'm good." She straightened her shoulders and smiled up at him. "Let's go." She would practice being in the present even though the past taunted her and the future loomed ahead like the dark pit of a basement.

Please don't break my heart.

Jay offered the crook of his arm, and she slid her hand around it. A light shiver went through her from the close proximity. "We're going to the farm first, right?" She had the feeling they wouldn't just be discussing reindeer-pulled sleighs.

"Yes. Mr. Parker is going to drive us there. We'll conduct our business and then move on to the real date. Is that okay?"

Her lips twitched. Of course he wouldn't stick to work, but Bebe would be lying if she claimed to be upset. "Yes. Sounds like a plan." She slid into the backseat, marveling at the amount of room.

Jahleel followed, stretching out his injured leg. "Then you aren't mad? I was hoping you wouldn't find me presumptuous."

Her eyebrows quirked. "Presumptuous?"

"What? Football players can't use big words?"

"Ha. If you fell into that stereotype, your parents would expire on the spot." She smiled at him. Only a strained laugh met her ears. "I'm sorry. I shouldn't have said that."

"Why not? It's true." He shrugged. "I'm used to their behavior. Or rather, my father's."

She yearned to offer a touch of comfort. Instead, she laced her fingers together. "Do you think it'll ever get better between the two of you?"

"Nah. Not as long as he values spouting Scripture more than establishing relationships."

"He has his moments. I've seen the way he looks at your mom. He obviously adores her."

Jay scoffed. "Where am I when this happens? He's usually frowning at her."

"A couple of years ago, she got pneumonia. Every time she coughed, a look of concern covered his face. It reminded me to have hope in marriage. That love could still be the way God intended." *Before men like Will ruined everything.*

Jahleel's eyes widened. "She had pneumonia?" His voice rose to a level that was not quite shouting but certainly not a normal decibel.

"You didn't know?" What had he missed staying in Texas? Had Reverend Walker forbade Jahleel from returning home, or had he just been so upset that coming back to Peachwood Bay was never an option?

"No," he gritted through his teeth. "Apparently no one bothered to tell me."

"Maybe they didn't want to disrupt your life. It *was* during football season."

"She's my *mother*, Bebe. It shouldn't have been a question. I would've been here in a heartbeat."

"How would they know that? You haven't been back in eight years. Do you even call them on the phone?" She clapped a hand over her mouth, eyes going wide. "I'm so sorry." The words were muffled behind her hand. She dropped her hand into her lap. "That is none of my business, and I have no right to speak on that."

Pain flashed in Jay's warm brown eyes. "You know," he said, rubbing his beard, "I always thought I was justified in leaving. Hearing lecture after lecture chafed worse than any astroturf burn. He never admitted to any wrongdoing. Instead he constantly placed the blame on me. When I told him I was going to make myself eligible for the NFL draft, he lost it. Called me everything but a child of God. All because

I refused to go to seminary so he could pass the church to me when he retired."

"Why didn't you want to be a pastor?" Jay had a wonderful understanding of the Bible, even when they were young.

"I'm not called. It's as simple as that."

"Perfect reason to say no."

"Not to Obadiah Walker." His lips twisted. "I've never been good enough."

Surely his father didn't really think that, yet short of asking him, Bebe couldn't refute Jay's comment. "Maybe all that matters is what God thinks."

"If my own father doesn't think much of me, how am I to be assured God would?" Deep pain reflected in his eyes.

This time Bebe didn't stop to think. She laced her fingers through his, and warmth spread up her arm. She gave his hand a squeeze, hoping he'd understand she was here for him. "God loves you unconditionally. That is a truth you can rest in."

A lump formed in Jay's throat. How could God love him unconditionally when his father didn't? The God his father taught was judgmental and harsh. Waiting to pierce with the sword those who fell short of His glory.

He thought of Remy, his Desperados' teammate from Louisiana. Remy spoke of a God who loved like a perfect father. Funny. He'd never thought Remy's words penetrated past all things football, but apparently they had.

"I don't know how to live like I believe that," he told Bebe. "Not when I have someone constantly reminding me that I'm not up to par."

"Don't compare the two. When we place man's limitations on God, His promises seem impossible. When we remember He is perfect, just, *and* loving, then His promises shine like the truth they are. Man will always fall short, but that doesn't mean we can't try to be better each and every day. Your dad is far from perfect, Jay, but you aren't perfect either. Both of you will make mistakes, but you can still choose to love and honor him with the capability God gives you. Only through God's strength will that be possible."

She squeezed his hand once more, and the vise around his chest lessened. How had she gotten so wise? "Thank you, Bebe."

"Anytime."

He held on to her hand, hoping she wouldn't pull away. The tenderness of her touch anchored him. Suddenly being in Peachwood Bay didn't seem like a death sentence but a hope of second chances.

By the time they arrived at the reindeer farm, the mood had lightened. Jahleel laughed as he exited the limo. Bebe had just reminded him of the time he'd run home screaming, convinced that the bogeyman was alive and real. He'd been seven at the time.

A log building stood sentry as land spread around them for miles. A red barn sat off to the right, most likely where the reindeer were. There was a picnic area in front of a food stand where kids milled around, chatting happily.

Jahleel held on to his cane and offered his arm once again. "Let's go inside. Looks like the log building is the main entrance."

"Right."

Bebe matched his pace, exclaiming over the smell of boiled nuts and cinnamon almonds. She pressed a hand to her stomach.

"Hungry?" he asked.

"Starving."

"We'll get something to eat once we're done here."

"Great." Relief turned her green eyes to moss.

Man, he wanted to kiss her.

Warmth greeted them as they walked into the main entrance. The sounds of "Jingle Bells" added to the cacophony of noise. There were reindeer products everywhere. It was almost like they had stepped into Santa's workshop. Snow globes, hats, T-shirts, and figurines lined the shelves throughout the store.

"Wow," Bebe whispered.

"No kidding."

He led them toward the checkout area. A robust man behind the cash register greeted them heartily. "Hello, there. How can I help you this fine day?"

"I'm Jahleel Walker, and this is Bebe Gordon."

"Ah, yes. I've been waiting for you."

He felt Bebe's stare as he shook the man's hand.

"I'm William Hammond. Welcome to the family farm." He turned to Bebe and shook her hand as well.

"Nice to meet you," she replied.

"Likewise. The reindeer are out in the barn, all ready to go." He rubbed the bald spot on his head. "My dad will be your guide and answer any questions you may have."

"Thank you." Jahleel ignored the tug from Bebe. "Do we just head on back?"

"Sure can."

As soon as they got outside, Bebe halted. "What are you up to?" She looked up at him.

"You'll find out soon enough." He gave her a small grin. "I promise you'll enjoy yourself."

She bit her lip and then slowly nodded. "Okay."

They resumed their pace. Jay's fingers wiggled as they got closer to the barn. Would she like his plan? Would she find it romantic? *Please let her find it romantic.* He'd taken care in planning today's activities because he wanted to show Bebe he was committed and not being casual with her heart. Surely caring how she felt about today was a step in that direction.

Bebe stopped suddenly when they entered the barn. The darkness surprised him, but his eyes finally adjusted. He bit back a grin.

A bright red sleigh was hooked up to eight reindeer. A fur blanket rested on the front of the sled. "Hello," he called out.

"Ho, ho, ho." An older gentleman came out of the shadows. He wore a red fur jacket held on by a black belt. His long white beard covered the center of it. "It's about time you got here, Bebe Gordon."

She gasped. "How do you know who I am?" She spared Jay a look, her eyes dancing with glee.

Yes! He knew she'd like this place.

"I know everyone." The man in red's cheeks bunched in merriment. "I hear you need a ride." He gestured toward the reindeer. "At your service, ma'am."

Bebe let go of Jay's arm and stepped forward. A look of pure delight stretched across her face. She glanced back at him and mouthed, *Santa!* Her eyes were wide with laughter. "Are these your helpers?" she asked the man.

"That they are. Couldn't make it anywhere without them. They get a little restless the closer we get to Christmas, so your man, Jahleel, here came to my rescue. The boys get to stretch their legs today while you get a tour."

"And what's your name?" Bebe asked.

"Why, I'm Santa, of course." He let out a laugh, clutching his belly. "Come on, come on, and get in the sleigh."

Jahleel held Bebe's hand as she climbed in. Then he carefully got in, sitting next to her. His knee ached, but this was totally worth it.

"The ride gets a little windy, so be sure to keep warm under the blanket," Santa called.

Jay grabbed the blanket, tucking it around them both.

"I can't believe this," Bebe whispered. She leaned close to his ear. "Thank you."

Goose bumps traveled across his nape. "You're welcome." He laced his fingers through hers and settled back as Santa led the way.

The wind picked up once they exited the barn, but Jay found that his beanie, the fur blanket, and Bebe pressed against his side kept him from feeling the cold. He glanced down at her, watching enchantment dance across her face.

As if she sensed his gaze, she looked up. "This is amazing," she said softly.

"Which part?" Because he still couldn't believe reindeer were pulling them across the Hammond farm as if they were going across snow in Alaska or some other snowy destination.

"All of it. Will Santa be the driver for the ball?"

Jay nodded. "He will."

"And will the fur blanket be there too?"

"Yes. He has two teams, so we can have two sleighs taking folks back and forth." Mr. Hammond's son apparently had a Santa outfit he could wear as well.

"I'm so excited about this." She paused, then squeezed his arm. "What happens when the ride ends?"

He could hear the underlying question. *What will happen to us?* He knew what he hoped for, but the logistics continued to evade him. "We trust God to work out the details." He swallowed, unsure of where that came from. Yet the words felt inherently right. As if the suggestion had been straight from God and not of his own might.

"So you want us to work out?"

"Yes." The answer came swiftly and without hesitation. Each day that Jay got to be around Bebe and spend time getting to know who she was now only confirmed that his feelings for her still ran deep. He loved Bebe Willabee Gordon.

She bit her lip. "Then I guess we know how to pray."

Jay hadn't done a whole lot of that prior to his injury, but he found himself lifting his voice to the Lord more and more.

Jay needed to get right with God so that he could be the man Bebe needed him to be. The man he hoped to become. No way he wanted a repeat of them separating without any contact. If God was willing and feelings continued to increase between them, he hoped they'd never part again.

"I'll pray right now." He squeezed his eyes shut, clenching them in an obvious way, but truly prayed.

When he opened his eyes, he found Bebe had done the same and was still praying. He placed a kiss on her forehead and thanked God for second chances.

Chapter
TWELVE

For once, Bebe didn't mind the early flag football game. Not when Jay sat next to her on the bleachers. He shouted enthusiastically every time Hope made a run. The little flutters that had been dancing in her heart seemed to morph into heart emojis in her eyes. His support of Hope was like a balm to her soul.

And so very dangerous.

How could she keep her heart guarded around a man who would spend his Saturday morning watching a bunch of second-graders play flag football? Not a single kid belonged to him, yet he showed up and cheered with the enthusiasm of a parent of multiple children. She peeked at him from under her Atlanta Falcons hat. A wide grin stretched on his face, emphasizing the crinkles that fanned out from his brown eyes. His cheeks were slightly red from the cold wind that blew.

He turned and caught her stare. "What?" He blew on his hands, then stuffed them into his jacket pockets.

"You really like football, huh?"

"You do too." He tapped the bill of her hat.

"But it's so early," she whined. Not that she minded the early day. Something about connecting with Jay over football had her grinning after the dramatic whine.

He chuckled. "Yeah, but your girl is good. She's the best player out here."

"That's bias talking." Still, pleasure filled her heart at the words.

"Nah, truth. I bet the coach has already told you that."

"Of course not. This is an equal-opportunity league." She pointed to the kid who seemed to be looking at insects versus the active play on the field. "Every kid gets an equal amount of playing time."

Jahleel rolled his eyes. "Well, take it from me. She's a natural."

"She's just having fun." It wasn't like Hope could become a professional player. Bebe just wanted her daughter to enjoy life, and football was part of that.

"That's the best part." He bumped her shoulder. "Come on. I know your football-lovin' self enjoys this."

"It's nine fifteen on a Saturday. There's a bed calling me and a Christmas movie waiting for me." But yes, she loved the game, even if all they did was pull a flag to end the play.

"How about this—after the game, we'll go to your place and watch all the Christmas movies you can stand."

"Deal." She shook the hand Jay offered and stilled. The warmth seemed to seep right into her heart. Suddenly the cold was no longer a factor. When had hanging out with Jay become an instinct and not even a question in her mind?

His gaze darkened and drifted down to her lips. Bebe gulped as her pulse picked up speed. Even though she'd been thinking more and more about the romantic feelings brewing between them, a flag football game was no place for a first kiss. Gently, she tugged at her hand.

Jay looked down and then guided her hand to his mouth. She inhaled sharply as his lips pressed gently against the back of it. *Good thing you didn't wear gloves.* He let go and turned back to the game. As if he hadn't just wrecked her and turned her into a jumbled ball of emotion.

Bebe stared across the field, trying to locate Hope and get her brain back on football. But her thoughts refused to switch gears. It was like every nerve in her hand had felt his soft touch. Her hand tingled, and goose bumps gleefully peppered her arm.

He hadn't kissed her on their date. She wasn't sure what had stopped him, because the evening had been absolutely perfect. Santa had driven them to an open field surrounded by oak trees covered in Spanish moss. A fire pit had been in the center of the field, enclosed by plush seating. How Jahleel had even coordinated something to that magnitude was beyond her. There had been food resting in a foil package on a grate above the fire pit and a cooler with the makings for s'mores.

Afterward, they had ridden back to the farm and arranged for Santa to come to the Christmas ball. Bebe had tried to get Mr. Hammond to show up as himself instead of as Santa, but Jay thought the kids would enjoy it. She just prayed Reverend Walker wouldn't be too upset by the jolly man's presence.

She jolted to attention as Hope ran past two defensive players. Her little legs pumped as she headed for the end zone. Bebe shot to her feet and began cheering. "Go, Hope!" The defensive players tried to catch her, but she had too much of a lead. She ran into the end zone and stopped, looking for the referee.

"See, I told you she has natural talent." Jay beamed with pride as Hope ran to the sidelines. "Way to go, Hope," he yelled, giving her two thumbs-up.

She waved enthusiastically and then guzzled down some water.

"Thank you for coming to her game." Bebe smiled at him.

"Since my parents moved to Florida, I'm the only one cheering her on. They would be here if they could, but it's just too far for weekend visits."

"Her father doesn't come visit at all?"

She shook her head.

Jay's jaw clenched, and he looked away. After a moment, he said, "I'm glad I could come." His hand reached for hers, squeezing it tightly. "Don't let her think it's her fault, Bebe."

"I won't." She gulped. "She knows she has a perfect Heavenly Father."

"I pray she remembers that."

"Me too."

They sat in silence for the remainder of the game. Bebe wondered what was going on in his brain. It was obvious that Will's behavior upset Jay, but he didn't say anything more about it. In fact, he hadn't spoken negatively about her ex at all. Still, he maintained a death grip on her hand until the referees blew the game whistle.

Hope ran over to the bleachers. "I made a touchdown! Did you see?"

"Sure did, pumpkin."

"You did awesome, Hope." Jay high-fived her. "I think you're my favorite player."

"Silly. You don't know anyone else here." Her cheeks puffed as if laughing at his comment.

"Yes, but I'm an expert when it comes to good football players."

A shy smile crossed her face. "You think I'm good?"

"The best one out there."

Hope threw her arms around his legs. "Thank you."

Jahleel patted her head while Bebe looked on.

The way her insides melted at the sight proved how much danger she was in of losing her heart to Jay once more. Bebe didn't know if that was a good thing or something to guard against. He'd apologized for the past and was so different from Will. Should she give in to her heart's desire or continue holding herself back?

⁓

Jahleel laughed along with Hope and Bebe. They were watching *Home Alone 2* while eating snacks. So far, they'd watched three movies, had lunch, and now ate popcorn. He couldn't remember when he'd had such a good time that didn't require a ton of money.

He frowned. Had he gotten pretentious? Was he throwing his money around instead of showing up and living? He stared at the TV, heart pounding. Every year he sent money home for his parents' birthdays, anniversary, and Christmas. Never once did he cross state lines to join them in celebration. Staying in Texas had been all about him. *His* need to maintain distance from his father. He'd always told himself that his mother didn't mind. That she understood their family dynamics.

How utterly selfish. His lip curled as he straightened up against the couch. Seeing Bebe parent Hope alone showed him how important it was to show up for the people you loved.

Lord, I messed up big time. Please forgive me for ignoring my mother just because my dad makes life difficult. Please help me know how to truly honor my parents and protect myself from the condemnation that my dad doles out. Amen.

Jahleel peeked at Bebe. They'd entered into some kind of relationship. What was he supposed to do about her? He couldn't leave her, but he needed a job. His savings wouldn't last forever. Should he go through with his business idea or not? Was he still being selfish by entering a relationship when he had no idea how it would work? He rubbed a hand across his face. If he left her now, he'd be a jerk of epic proportions.

Unease fluttered in his chest. He couldn't mess this up. Bebe meant too much to him, and Hope deserved someone who would cheer her on every day, not just at random. Jahleel gulped. *What do I do, Lord?*

"You okay?" Bebe whispered.

He nodded, not sure what to say.

Her eyes searched his. Slowly, she shook her head. "You're not."

"We can talk later." He made a point of glancing toward Hope, who lay on the floor with her blanket.

"You want to leave, don't you?" Bebe tensed.

"No." *I don't want to hurt you.*

She stared at him, steel and determination stiffening her expression. She didn't believe him.

Jahleel leaned toward her, his lips by her ear. "I don't want to hurt you. I'm sitting here realizing I haven't been the best son, and I'm afraid I won't be the best boyfriend either."

She turned, her lips impossibly close to his. "Is that all?"

"Isn't that enough?" He snorted.

"What matters is how you act now that you've realized your faults." She cupped his cheek. "I don't need perfect. I just need you to be here."

"What happens when I go back to Texas?" His breath suspended as he waited for her answer.

"What do you want to happen?"

"I want us to be together."

Yearning darkened her eyes. "Really?"

"Really."

She bit her lip. "I've been praying, and I've been thinking about us, like you suggested. I think we should continue to take it one day at a time. Let's see where God leads us."

That almost seemed too easy. In the past, not being able to commit right then and there was a point of contention. *But y'all have matured.* Still . . . "Just like that?"

"If we both want to see where this goes, we'll eventually figure out all the details."

"Okay." He blew out a breath. He could live with that. He'd been telling her God would give them the details. Now it was Jahleel's turn to remember that and lean on God's understanding.

Bebe caressed his cheek, then dropped her hand. He captured it, placing a kiss on her palm. Lacing his fingers with hers, he turned his attention back to the movie.

He sat there, holding her hand in his, watching Hope crack up at the robbers' antics. This could be his life permanently. Sitting with the woman who captured his heart and the little girl who earned her own spot there. He wanted to be the best man possible for their sakes.

He wasn't yet sure what role he would fill in Hope's world. She didn't have a father present, but he didn't want to step on another man's toes. Who knew the reason Will kept his distance? Granted, Jahleel wanted to punch the man in the face every time he thought of him, but maybe one day Will would be a good father to Hope.

Until then . . .

Well, he'd keep praying for God's guidance.

THIRTEEN

Will's ringtone sounded, and Bebe groaned. She was not ready for any kind of conversation with Will. *Are you ever?* But maybe he'd called to speak to Hope.

"Hello?"

"Lucille."

She rolled her eyes. "What's up?"

"I need to talk to you."

Yeah, she'd figured that out from the phone call. *Chill, don't let him rile you up already.* "I'm listening."

"Actually, could we meet at Sam's?"

Wait, he was at the diner? "You're here?" she whispered. Will hadn't visited Peachwood Bay since he met her parents when they were dating. Her breath caught. Was he finally going to take an interest in Hope?

"Yes. But could you come alone?"

She frowned. Why didn't he want to see Hope? "I'm not sure I can find a babysitter on such short notice. Besides, don't you want to see your daughter?"

"If you know what's good for you, you'll find someone to watch her. We *have* to talk."

She straightened in her seat. "Are you threatening me?"

"No, Lucille." Exasperation tinged his voice. "Just get down here."

"Fine. Give me ten minutes." She hung up and immediately texted May.

BEBE
You busy?

MAY
'I'm in Atlanta with Ryan. Y? What's up?

BEBE
Never mind. I'll ttyl.

MAY
K.

Rosa and her family had gone on a cruise for their winter vacation. Who could she ask to watch over her daughter? *Jahleel?* She bit her lip and opened a text to him.

BEBE
Are you home?

JAY
Where else would I be? Everything ok?

BEBE
I have to meet Will for some mysterious reason. Can you watch Hope?

Jahleel's picture flashed as an incoming call.

"Hey," she said in greeting.

"What does he want?" Concern etched his words.

Bebe leaned back against the couch, staring mindlessly at the Christmas tree. "I have no idea." She shrugged. "He told me to come alone. He's acting really strange."

"Do you think you'll be safe with him?"

She frowned. Should she mention the threat? Well, it wasn't really one. Was it? "He's never hurt me before." *Not physically, at least.*

"I don't like this, Bebe."

"I don't either, but maybe he's ready to step into his role as a dad." That spark of hope hadn't been doused yet.

A sigh met her ears. "God willing. Do you want me to come over there?"

"No way. I can bring her by so you can rest your knee."

"I *can* walk, Bebe."

She smirked at the irritation in his voice. It reminded her of when they were younger and how he always tried to present his best front, then got frustrated when life happened. "I know, but you're still recovering. We'll be over in five."

"See you then."

"Hope!" Bebe yelled as soon as the call ended.

A few moments later, the footsteps sounded. Hope walked into the living room. "Yes, Mama?"

"I have to go somewhere real fast. Mr. Walker's going to watch you until I get back, okay?"

Hope nodded. "Am I going over to his house?"

"Yes."

"Can I bring Bunny with me?"

"Sure, pumpkin."

Bebe gathered her things and then escorted Hope next door. As soon as she stepped onto the porch, the Walkers' front door opened. Jay stood there in a gray sweater, looking gorgeous. She inhaled, wondering why his looks got to her in this moment.

He smiled. "Hey, Hope. *The Grinch* is on."

"Cartoon or humans?"

"Cartoon."

"Oh goodie!" Hope grinned and dashed inside.

Jay stepped closer to Bebe, his brow furrowed. "Are you sure you'll be okay by yourself? My mama is home, and we can leave Hope with her. I can be there as a just-in-case."

Her heart melted at the offer. "I really appreciate that, but I think I'll be okay. You could say a prayer."

"Already done."

The strength emanating from him made her want to lean against him and enjoy the safety of his arms. But she didn't want to fall apart before meeting Will. Instead, she took a step back and gave him a soft smile. "Thanks, Jahleel."

"Hurry back."

Her pulse fluttered. With a small wave, she headed for her car. Ten minutes later, she pulled up to Sam's Shack, the smell of fried seafood greeting her. Too bad meeting Will had ruined any appetite she had for Sam's food.

Bebe walked into the wood building that resembled a beach shack. The dimness made it a little difficult to see, but Will stuck out like a sore thumb. He was the only one wearing a suit. She snorted and headed toward the table way in the back. His eyes widened a little when he noticed her.

He stood. "Lucille." He slid his hands down his slacks.

Something was very wrong. She swallowed. "Will." She pulled out one of the wooden chairs to sit on.

"Thanks for meeting me."

"Mm-hmm."

"I'm sure you're wondering what this is all about."

Yes, because every alarm in her body was sounding. She didn't know whether she needed to fight or flee. "I am."

He gulped. "It's like this. Angie's pregnant."

Of course. For some reason, the news didn't faze her. She'd figured it would happen sooner or later. The fact that they managed to be together this long and not have a child was the real surprise. Unease snaked through her gut. "Congrats."

Thank goodness she didn't feel heartache or bitterness. Maybe she was finally over the trauma that was Will Gordon.

He tapped his fingers against the table. "I can't afford to make the same mistakes with Angie that I did with you."

"You mean like cheating on her with your secretary?"

He winced. "No, I was thinking about Hope."

"Wait, what? Did you cheat on Angie and get another woman pregnant as well?"

"No!" he said loudly, then lowered his voice again. "Good grief, Lucille. I've learned my lesson, all right?"

A server approached their table. Will waved him off, so Bebe kept her desire for a tall glass of water to herself.

"Then what is this all about? You just want me to know she's pregnant? Prepare Hope?" Now that she thought about it, Bebe had no idea how her daughter would respond to this bit of news.

"Um, no. I, uh . . ." He blew out a breath. "Angie's not like you, Lucille. She needs me more, and I . . . I don't want to mess this up."

He kept saying that. What did he mean? He'd already married Angie and claimed he hadn't cheated. He was already doing better in his second marriage than when they'd been together.

"What does this have to do with me? With Hope?" Then it dawned on her. "Do you want her for Christmas after all?" Dread and hope mixed within her. Her darling girl would love to spend time with him, but Bebe would be miserable without her.

"Uh . . ." His Adam's apple bobbed. "Not exactly."

"New Year's?"

"No. I don't want her." He raked a hand over his hair.

"But you just said . . ." *He didn't want to repeat his mistakes, right?*

He rubbed the back of his neck. "I'm making a mess of things." He met her gaze head on. "I'm turning over my rights." He leaned down and pulled some papers out of his briefcase.

Her heart thudded in her chest. "I don't understand."

"Like I was saying, I need to devote my time to Angie. She needs me. So I am signing over my parental rights." He pushed the papers toward her.

Bebe stared down in confusion, skimming the paperwork. She gasped and looked up. "You don't want to be Hope's father anymore?" Was he serious?

He winced. "It's not like that. She has you, and I'm sure you'll marry again someday. If you do, he can adopt Hope, and she can have a real family. Angie . . . well, Angie needs me to devote all my time to our family."

"You can *not* be serious. You don't just get to check some box and stop being Hope's father, Will. After all, she has half of your DNA!" She drew in a breath, placing her hands against the tabletop. "You can't just give up your rights, Will." *He can't.*

"I actually can. I've already talked to a lawyer. All you have to do is sign in agreement, and it'll be a done deal." He gulped. "Um, it will also stop child support."

Of course it would.

"But I'd be willing to set up an account for her." He shrugged. "I could still give you some money if you aren't doing so well."

"Why? That's something a *father* would do." She folded her arms across her chest.

"Look, Lucille, I'm married and have to take into account my wife's wishes. Surely you understand that."

This was rich. This . . . *bozo* cheated on her, and now he was appealing to her for understanding so he could abdicate the responsibility of being a father to Hope? To parent some unborn child like her precious baby hadn't existed for seven years already?

"You'll follow Angie's wishes to the detriment of your child?"

Sorrow filled his eyes. "Please just sign the papers."

An ache filled her throat as hot tears welled against her eyes. Time seemed to stop as she stared at the paperwork. How could she do this? Sign papers agreeing that he would no longer be her child's father? It was just . . . *wrong.*

"It would make this easier, *Bebe,* please."

Her eyes shot to his.

"I'll make sure she won't want for anything," he said.

"Except the presence of her father."

Will remained silent.

"You know what?" She scooted her chair back. "I can't do this. I can't look her in the eye and say I agreed to this. Let the courts solve it."

She walked away, heart breaking for her precious child.

The next day, Jahleel stood next to Bebe in Wal-Mart, staring at the karaoke machines. "You really think this is a good idea? I can't see many people wanting to do karaoke."

The idea of karaoke at a Christmas ball was a little weird to him. But that was the last thing on his mind. He wanted to know what had happened with Will and erase the sadness that clung to Bebe like tinsel on a Christmas tree.

"Why not? The whole point of this is to come together and enjoy ourselves. What's better than singing Christmas songs for karaoke? The congregation will probably join in. Even your dad can't argue with some heavenly worship."

He laughed, throwing his head back. "Obadiah Walker can argue about everything. But you might be right."

"Good. Then let's test this out." She nudged him with a wink, but still the smile didn't reach her eyes.

"You got jokes, girl. I am *not* doing karaoke." He didn't want to hear his voice or do some kind of song and dance.

"Come on, Jay. It'll be fun. You can sing the song with the hippo."

His heart stuttered. It wasn't fair that she could bat those eyes and he'd willingly do her bidding. "Bebe," he groaned.

"You'll love it. I promise." She grinned and picked the machine off the shelf.

"Let me get that for you."

She stared at him pointedly. "Yeah, because I'm the one holding a cane." She shook her head. "It's not that heavy."

"Fine." Maybe they should've grabbed a cart to lug that around. "Is there anything else we need?"

"Yes. We need to head to the craft section next. We need items for the kids to make ornaments, and this year we'll also do a reindeer hot chocolate craft."

"Then I'm grabbing a cart." He maneuvered around the store with his cane until he found an empty cart and returned to the spot where he'd left Bebe.

When Bebe had first suggested the reindeer hot chocolate, Jahleel thought she was slightly unhinged. But he had to admit, a pack of hot chocolate decorated as a reindeer was a cute gift and something the kids would enjoy.

"Ready now. Lead the way." He gestured ahead of him.

Bebe placed the karaoke machine in the cart, then headed down the aisle. She looked adorable in her white sweater that fell to mid-thigh, where his eyes couldn't help but follow the candy canes decorating her leggings. She looked festive, and he just wanted to wrap her in his arms.

It was official. He was a goner. What else made sense? Jahleel usually hated shopping, and now he was actually enjoying himself.

They hit the craft aisle, filling their basket with eyeballs, red felt balls, and material for reindeer ears. Fortunately, the store had lots of materials to make your own ornaments. Next, they hit one of the food aisles to grab hot chocolate. All the while, they laughed and joked.

He kissed Bebe's forehead. "This has been a lot of fun."

"You seem shocked." Her green eyes twinkled with amusement.

"We are in a store."

She grinned. "Still allergic to shopping?"

"Yes, ma'am. That's why I have a personal shopper."

"That is so sad. A grown man who can't even shop for himself."

He couldn't tell if she was teasing him or something else. "What can I say? The comforts money will bring."

"Do you think that's true?" A V formed on her brow.

"What?" He stared at her. There seemed to be some downward shift, but he wasn't sure why. Or what had caused the somber mood. Was it related to Will and their conversation yesterday?

"Do you truly think money brings comfort? That it's a better substitute for presence?"

"Presents? Like those boxes under a tree?"

"No." She huffed. "I think people believe they can throw money around instead of showing up. You see people who will chase after money until it consumes them. Never satisfied with the 'comforts' it brings." She used air quotes on *comforts*.

Now they were getting somewhere. "*People* or your exhusband?" he asked softly.

Bebe swallowed. *Ah-ha.*

"I'm not like Will. Yes, I believe that money brings comfort. I was able to hire a limo for us on our date. I am funding everything for the Christmas ball. But I'm not absent. I'm active in the committee, and I think you know that."

"I know." She sniffed.

"Do you want to talk about it?"

A tear trailed down her face, and his gut twisted. Did he still need to prove himself to Bebe, or was there something more? Because here he was, shopping for Christmas crafts. If that didn't tell her his commitment to the ball—to *her*—he didn't know what would.

"Will doesn't want to be Hope's father anymore."

He jerked backward. "What?"

"You heard me correctly." She swiped at the tear on her face. "He wants to sign his rights over so that he can raise a new baby with his wife."

"The woman he cheated on you with?"

She nodded.

He prayed for wisdom. "Are you still in love with him?"

"No." Bebe shook her head vehemently. "I hate how he's ignored Hope. I hate that he cheated on me. I absolutely do *not* want him back. But I don't know how I can look my daughter in the face and tell her I agreed to let her dad escape responsibility."

"I'm sure you prayed about it?"

She nodded.

"Then all you can do is let God lead you. You can't make him be a parent, even if that's exactly what he is."

"I just don't know how I could've been so wrong about him. It makes me question everything."

"Like us?" he asked.

"Yes," she whispered.

He tipped her chin up. "I'm not going anywhere."

"But you are. You have to go back to Texas eventually."

"True, but I'll be back." Because he wanted her in his life for the everyday activities like shopping and to be there to show Hope that she wasn't fatherless. Whether that meant Bebe allowed him to step into that role or he continued to point her to their Heavenly Father. Regardless, he knew without a doubt that Bebe Gordon held his heart. "I'm not leaving us. But I do have a home there I just can't abandon."

"I know, Jahleel." Her honeyed voice seemed to caress him.

"Then trust me when I say I'll be back. I'm not leaving never to return. I just have to make sure my next steps lead me to a secure job."

She gasped. "You're not going back to the Stars?"

"No." He slid his hands into his pockets, wishing the heartache away.

Her mouth dropped open. "But you *love* football."

"Ryan doesn't believe the knee will allow me to fulfill my contract. And now, I have other priorities. Much prettier ones." He winked.

"Then what next?"

"Time will tell."

She studied him, then nodded.

"What's next on the list, boss?" He pushed the cart, thankful it could take his full weight, since his cane rested inside it.

"Door prizes."

"All right."

As she led the way once more, Jahleel sent a prayer upward.

Lord, please help her trust that I'm not leaving her. Help her know that I want to be with her and that nothing will change that.

Then tell her you love her.

He sighed. Was that really the best thing right now? Will had dealt a heavy blow. Jahleel didn't want to add more weight to the worries already bogging her down. Besides, he didn't want to say the words and then leave for Texas, even if he planned to return. It would probably cause unnecessary angst.

No. It was best to wait. Today's business was making sure she could process Will's decision. Tomorrow would worry about itself.

FOURTEEN

May handed Bebe a cup of hot chocolate. "So what are you going to do?"

"I don't know." Bebe sipped her drink. The whipped cream blended smoothly with May's homemade cocoa recipe. She looked around at her friend's cozy cottage, festive with Christmas decorations. She had a small Christmas tree sitting on the coffee table with origami cranes hanging from it. The larger tree in front of the window held glass ornaments May had been collecting since she was a young girl. She and her folks always went to local Christmas markets to find them.

"What do you want to do?" May asked.

"Is it ridiculous that the idea of moving to Texas has been replaying in my head?" The words tore from her lips. She stared, stunned, as the truth hit her.

She didn't want to part from Jay. She'd been praying for their relationship, for God to be in the details, all the while expecting Jay to move to Peachwood Bay. But every time she had the thought, it was followed by the understanding that this was an unrealistic expectation. Jay had never wanted to remain in Peachwood Bay, and if she were honest, that had never been her dream either.

"Ah, you didn't know you wanted to, huh?" May smirked.

Bebe pressed a hand to her forward. "I'm crazy, aren't I?"

"Depends on the reason behind the want."

Bebe stared into her mug. Her heart pounded as dream after dream flitted through her mind. Despite her prayers to stay present and not jump into the future, she couldn't discount the very real desire to make a home with Jay and Hope. One filled with flag football Saturdays, football Sundays, and joy the rest of the week.

"Bebe?"

"Just thinking." She met May's gaze. "I let him go to college without a backward glance. Okay, not completely true, but I didn't put up a fight. I don't want to make the same mistake now. I see a future with us, always have."

"Then listen to your heart, girlfriend. And, of course, talk to God."

"I have been. I'm just not sure how much of the response is my own wishes or His leading."

"Hmm, I know that feeling. Have you talked this over with Jay?"

She grimaced. "Kind of? We've said we want to be together, and he's promised he won't leave me for good again."

May grinned. "Those are some big steps. I knew you guys were meant to be!"

Bebe chuckled.

"I'm so happy for you. Have you considered looking at jobs out there?"

Bebe's stomach roiled at the thought. "No. It's all just coming together in my mind."

"My mom always says not to quit a job without having another one." May wrinkled her nose.

"I . . . right. That should be a simple thing to look into." Yet the thought of leaving Georgia and going to Texas filled her with slight panic. Was she doing the right thing? Was this the next move? Or would Jay think it weird that she was contemplating moving to Texas already?

What was preventing her from jumping at the prospect of moving? She would miss Peachwood Bay, but she didn't have any real ties here. Her folks let her rent their home—that had been more at Bebe's insistence than theirs—so they could either rent it out again or sell it. But she and Jahleel hadn't even said the *L*-word. How could she just move to Texas without talking to him about it?

She pressed a hand against her stomach. "Does this all seem too fast to you?" Surely May would be honest.

"I might be the wrong person to ask because I'm thinking of moving too." May took a sip of her hot chocolate as if they were having a normal, mundane conversation.

"Excuse me? What on earth are you taking about?" May couldn't leave. Who would Bebe do life with?

"Ryan's based in Nashville. It's kind of hard to have a relationship if I'm eight hours away."

We're all mad here. "How do you know he's worth it? What do you even know about him?"

"I know he makes me laugh, and you know how much I like to laugh."

Bebe studied her friend. "You're going to move to Nashville to laugh? Do you hear yourself?"

"I'm not tying the knot tomorrow, girl, so calm down. The only reason I've stayed in Peachwood Bay is because I'm comfortable." May shrugged. "My parents moved five years ago and love Atlanta. Moving to Nashville doesn't make the distance to Atlanta any farther. It's literally the same amount of time. I'm just trying to be closer to Ryan to see if we have what it takes to make it. If not, then at least I tried."

If not, then at least I tried. Why did that feel like a punch to the gut? "May," Bebe whispered.

"You've stopped living, Bebe. You let Will steal your joy and trap you in a town you're not committed to."

"I . . . I love Peachwood Bay."

"You do, but you and I both know you're merely passing time here. Now it looks like the reason for your waiting has arrived. Jay wants to be with you, and you're waiting for the other shoe to drop."

May was right. Bebe was scared to live. Scared to do anything that would put her heart at risk for more heartache. *But God never promised this life would be easy or that your heart wouldn't break.*

"I don't know how to live anymore," she admitted. "And how do I know he won't leave me again?" *Or divorce me like Will?*

"Because this time he told you he wouldn't. Plus, you've been checking in with God. You didn't do that before, right?"

Bebe shook her head.

"I'm sure you can figure out the right path before Christmas gets here and that man leaves. You'll both want answers by that point."

Bebe nodded. She already wanted answers, but Jay had pointed out that she didn't need to know the end to start. Maybe going out with him, shopping with him, and watching movies with him and Hope had all been the first steps in learning how to live and trust again. Not just trusting another man but trusting herself and that she was looking toward the Lord as her source.

"Just keep on taking baby steps. Oh, and look for a job." May grinned.

"I don't want to live far away from you." Bebe poked her lip out, wanting to throw an adult-sized tantrum. Why did life have to be so difficult?

"At least we'd both be moving. If I stayed here, you would be farther from me in San Antonio than if I move to Nashville."

Bebe sighed. "Fine."

"I have some frequent-flyer miles." May put an arm around her. "I'll visit." She squeezed Bebe's hand. "We went to different colleges and managed to stay the best of friends. We can handle you moving to Texas."

"Still. I'll miss you." But May was right. Their friendship had stood the test of time, it could handle a move. *If that was what Jay wanted as well.*

"Here, I'll get my laptop, and we'll look for jobs." May got up and headed for her bedroom.

Bebe closed her eyes. *Lord, I need a sign. I'm talking about a loud, lightning-striking type of sign. I know You want my trust, and You have it. I just don't trust myself. I want to trust I hear Your voice and not my own. Help me to know it's You. Please, please help me.*

She let out a yelp when she opened her eyes. May was staring at her, wearing a headband with reindeer antlers made of felt. "Why didn't you make some noise coming back in here? And what's with the antlers?"

"Hello, you were praying." May grinned mischievously. "The antlers were in case I scared you."

Bebe chuckled.

"I pulled up the San Antonio school district. Of course, I have no clue where Jay lives. He could live in the suburbs or something. If you want to be near him but not tell him that you're looking yet, ask Mrs. Walker. She'll go crazy with excitement."

His mama had been the first to call out the rift between them. "You're probably right."

"That's because I always am." May winked.

As they searched through the listings, the butterflies in Bebe's stomach slowly settled down. There were a few kindergarten openings in the district. One even advertised for a start after the New Year. Could that be a sign from God that moving to Texas was the right move?

With a prayer, she waited for apprehension to fill her, but rightness took its place. Figuring it couldn't hurt to see what happened, Bebe let May help her fill out the application. At the last page, May paused. "You ready to hit submit?"

Was she? Bebe pictured Jahleel. The way he had made snowman cookies with her and Hope. The laughter they'd all shared while watching Christmas movies. The way he hugged her as if he never wanted to let go.

"Yes, hit submit."

❧

"Are you sure, Walker?"

"Yes, Marty. I want to retire."

After talking to Ryan about his recovery progress last night, Jahleel had formally made his decision. He'd have Marty make a statement to announce his retirement after the season was officially over. Being here in Peachwood Bay had made him realize that achieving a dream meant nothing if he had no one to share it with. He'd played for the NFL for eight years, and not once had his mother or father attended a game. Not to mention that he'd missed out on the best relationship he'd ever had.

He'd come to grips with his past mistakes, and now he was looking forward to a future with much promise. He wasn't yet sure how long he and Bebe would have a long-distance relationship, but he trusted God would put everything in place with His perfect timing.

"You don't want to try for a broadcasting career?" Marty asked. "I'm sure I could find you a spot on someone's show or even get you your own."

The offer wasn't even tempting. "Nah, Marty. My priorities are different now."

"Georgia messing with your mind?"

Jay chuckled. "No. It righted my mind."

His agent sighed. "What are you going to do after retirement?"

"Lead a normal life."

"Good luck, then, Walker."

"Thanks, Marty."

Jahleel hung up and stood. His stomach rumbled, reminding him that it was lunchtime. He headed for the kitchen. Now that he could walk without added pain, cooking had become his stress reliever. If his mom was home, she'd often join him. It had been great reconnecting with her again. This time when he went back to Texas, he wouldn't be a stranger. And maybe, somehow, he could convince her to fly out and visit.

The sound of the Temptations' Christmas album greeted his ears as he neared the kitchen. He stopped short in the doorway. His mom and dad were dancing, twirling around the room and grinning from ear to ear. His father sang along as he spun his mom out and then wrapped her in his arms.

Jahleel's cheeks flushed at the intimacy of the moment. Not once had he ever wanted a marriage like his parents', always assuming his father was too harsh, too unbearable to live with. Only now he was wondering if that was his own view of the man. Because this . . . this was something he hadn't seen before.

Or did I just ignore the good, too focused on the bad?

Bebe had shared with him the moments his father had preached something that lifted her spirits and reminded her God was her source for all things. Other patrons seemed to take his bluster as all bark and no bite. So what was he missing that others were seeing?

The Reverend looked up and paused mid-stride. "Jahleel."

His mom whirled around. "Hey, son. Hungry?"

"Uh . . ." Why couldn't he speak? He was too old to be embarrassed by his parents' display of affection, except he couldn't recall seeing it before. *Or had he blocked those memories?*

He shook his head.

"Didn't know your dad had some moves, huh?" His mom's eyes twinkled, glowing underneath her blue eye shadow. "We took dancing classes a couple of years ago."

After she'd recovered from pneumonia? "That's neat." *Neat? That's all you can say?* "I just came in to make some lunch."

"I got Sam's, if you want some," his father offered.

Jahleel paused in shock. This was the nicest thing his father had said to him since he'd been back. "What did you get?" Maybe this was the olive branch he'd been praying for.

"Three oyster specials."

His mouth watered in anticipation. "Thank you. I'd like that."

His father grabbed a to-go container out of the oven and handed it over. Jahleel dipped his head in thanks and headed for the table. He stood there for a moment. Maybe he should go eat in his room? Leave his parents to their dancing?

He looked up at the sound of a throat clearing.

"Have a seat, son. Maybe we can talk."

"Good idea," his mother said. She tapped his father's shoulder. "I'll go work in the back."

Jahleel sat down, unease gathering in the pit of his stomach. What could his father have to say? He wasn't up for a battle of wits or condemnation. All he wanted to do was eat his food in peace. *Lord, please be in the midst of this conversation, and thank You for this food.*

He took a bite of the fried oysters. He'd get at least one bite in before the lecture started.

"Need some hot sauce?" his father asked.

"Please." Jahleel licked his lips. His father wouldn't make enjoying his food easy. Still, the oysters, hush puppies, and crinkle fries called to him. "Ketchup too, please."

His father placed the condiments on the table, then sat across from him. "How's your knee doing?"

"Better." He ate a fry.

"Will you make a full recovery?"

Did his dad care? *Lord, please keep my preconceived notions out of my head and let me hear him out.* "I should."

"Good."

Silence permeated the air.

"Is the team saving your spot?"

"No. I'm retiring." He watched his father for a reaction.

Surprise filled the Reverend's eyes. "But you just said you'll make a full recovery." His brow furrowed. "Do you need better physical therapy? A new doctor?"

Maybe his father *did* care. "The injury was too severe for me to make it back on the field. A full recovery simply means I won't have a limp. But more than that, I have different priorities now." Just thinking about Bebe made him want to grin, but he curbed the impulse, lest his father think Jay was making light of their conversation.

His father rubbed his gray chin. "Will you be staying in Texas?"

"Most likely." He wanted to. It was home to him now, but if Bebe wanted to stay in Peachwood Bay, wouldn't he move here? He would *not* leave her again.

"Can't imagine you staying here, that's for sure."

"Yeah, I get it. I'm never around." Jay's jaw clenched.

"Do you hear insults all the time?"

Unfair. His father loved insulting him. To insinuate that it was all Jay was a bit ridiculous. A lot ridiculous. He drew in a deep breath to speak.

"You don't fit here," his father said quietly. "Never really have."

Jahleel's mouth dropped open. "But you've always pressured me about staying here. *Always*." That wasn't his imagination.

He could bring up hordes of conversations from the past to prove his point.

"I know." His father rubbed his chin again. "I admit I was a little—"

"Zealous?"

"Demanding."

Jahleel hid a sigh. He wanted to interrupt and argue, but hadn't he asked God to help give him a new perspective?

"What I want to understand is why." Jahleel studied his father. "Why was I never good enough?"

His father dropped his head, looking at the dining room table. Jay watched, waiting for the other shoe to drop. Would he yell? Tell Jahleel it was all in his head? *Lord, please, help us get the truth out. I'm tired of feeling less-than, and it all started with him.*

"Son, I was never holding a measuring stick."

"Really? Because you've told me Walkers are always preachers. Walkers respect the Lord. Walkers wouldn't sell their soul to play football. If that's not a measuring stick, I don't know what is."

His father's Adam's apple bobbed. "You're right. I said those things."

"And you believed them?" Jahleel made it a question even though his heart knew the answer. Still, he was trying.

"Yes, I did believe them."

"Did?" His brows rose. "What changed? And if you changed your mind, then why no word from you?"

"You could have always called us."

"How was I supposed to know you wanted any communication with me when you're the one who kicked me out and told me never to return?"

His father sighed. "The moment your mother told me she was pregnant, I was elated." He looked Jay square in the eye. "There wasn't a day that went by that I didn't dream of plans for you and me. From studying the Word together to going fishing, teaching you how to sail. If a man ever had a moment of hopes and wishes for his future son, I had them too."

"So what happened? Because all I remember from you was condemnation. Even when I showed up here injured, you were still throwing shade my way, as if it were my own fault I blew out my knee."

"Your mother sat me down." His father paused. "Were you aware she had pneumonia?"

Jahleel nodded. "Bebe told me. It would've been nice to know at the time of her illness."

"I refused to call you, and she was too sick to do so."

The words felt like a blow to the gut. Nevertheless, he motioned for his father to continue.

"I honestly thought it would take her life. I've never prayed so hard, and God answered. She turned the corner for the better and was home a week later. When she came home, she sat me down. Told me I'd let stuff in my past harden my heart."

That Jay could believe one hundred percent. But what stuff in his father's past had embittered him?

"At first I didn't want to hear what she had to say. But after that, I started hearing conversations around the church. Not because I was purposely eavesdropping, but I'm a quiet walker."

That was true. Jahleel could never sneak up on his father, but Obadiah Walker made it his life duty to do so to others.

"There were comments about me being a difficult man to please and that I was a fire-and-brimstone type of preacher."

"Is that not who you want to be? Or who you thought you were?" Jay asked.

"No. I love the Lord with all my heart, but I grew up with a man who believed in not sparing the rod, and I don't mean he disciplined me with a right mindset. I was beat."

Jay's mouth dried.

"I promised never to lay a hand on my son, but I think not coming to grips with my childhood tainted my mindset anyway. I beat you with my words, and I . . ." His father swallowed, his eyes looking glassy. "I'm sorry. I'm trying. Your mother has been calling me out on it more and more. She even apologized for being an enabler and not saying something sooner."

Jahleel blinked. He'd never considered his mother an enabler, but maybe when he was a child, he'd wished she would speak up for him. "I'm sorry you went through that. I didn't know."

"I would've never been comfortable sharing before now," his dad admitted.

"So why now?"

"I want to fix the rift I created."

"I've been praying for an olive branch," Jahleel admitted.

"So have I." His father's mouth ticked up a tiny bit at the corner. "I'm sorry, son."

Jay nodded slowly, releasing a breath. He'd never thought to hear those words come out of Obadiah Walker's mouth. "Thank you for saying that."

His father stood. "I should've never kicked you out. You've done great things in your career, and I hope you're a first ballot Hall of Famer."

"Time will tell."

"I understand you wanting to go back to Texas, but know you'll always be welcome here."

A lump formed in his throat. "I appreciate that. And, um." He stood so he could look his father in the eye. "You're always welcome to visit me in San Antonio. I have plenty of guest bedrooms . . . Dad."

His father blinked rapidly. Jahleel thought he saw a tear slide down his cheek, but the Reverend turned away before Jay could search any further. Instead, he raised a hand in acknowledgment and trudged down the hall.

What just happened?

Somehow, someway, he and his dad had just had a heart-to-heart that didn't leave Jahleel feeling bitter but instead feeling like he'd received a Christmas miracle.

He grinned. *Thank You, Lord. All praise and glory to You, all day and every day.*

Chapter

FIFTEEN

Winter vacation had officially started. Bebe smiled as she parked in front of her carport. Hope jumped out of the car, excitement on her face. She skipped to the front door.

"Can we make hot chocolate with marshmallows, Mama?"

"Sure, pumpkin." She unlocked the door. "But go put your backpack up and change out of your school clothes first."

Jay was supposed to come over so they could resume their holiday movie watching. Up tonight were *The Polar Express* and *Elf.*

"Okay." Hope skipped down the hall to her bedroom.

Bebe chuckled and set her bag on the kitchen counter. Her cell rang, and she shifted, pulling it out of her purse. *Texas?* Who did she know there?

"Hello?"

"May I speak to Lucille Gordon?"

She winced. "Speaking."

"Ms. Gordon, this is Judy Simpson from the San Antonio Independent School District Human Resources Department. I'm calling regarding your application."

Bebe's stomach lurched as if a flock of geese had just taken off.

"You currently reside in Peachwood Bay, Georgia, correct?"

"Yes, ma'am."

"Will you be in San Antonio over the holidays?"

"Uh, no."

"Then would you be able to do an interview via a video call?"

"Yes. I'd be happy to."

"Great. Would you be available Monday at two?"

She gulped. "I would." Was this really happening? What were the odds of actually getting called for an interview for the first job she applied for? *You mean the* only *job you applied for.*

"Fantastic. One last question. Would you be able to move over the holiday vacation and start work the day after the New Year?"

Bebe's legs wobbled, and she grabbed the counter to steady herself. Should she say yes when she hadn't even had a chance to talk to Jay about a possible move yet? Then again, she couldn't make Ms. Simpson wait for her to have a conversation with her boyfriend.

"As long as I'm able to give appropriate notice to my current job, I don't see how that would be a problem." But could she pack and do all the other things required before then?

"Great. The kindergarten teacher you'd be replacing if you got the job is going on maternity leave for the rest of the school year. Although there's an assistant, the class is quite large and does so much better with a two-man team."

"That makes sense. Does that mean this is a temporary job?"

Could she move out to Texas knowing she'd be job hunting in the summer? *It's one interview. It's not like you can't apply to more than one place.*

"The teacher has until the end of the school year to inform us if she is indeed coming back for the next term. Then we'd be able to tell you for sure if it was temporary or yours."

"Thank you for letting me know."

"Misty Baker will be the one conducting the interview. I'll let her know you're able to speak to her Monday."

"Thank you."

"You're welcome. Have a good holiday."

"You too."

Bebe set her cell on the counter. They wanted to interview her? Monday? And have her move at the beginning of the year? What would Jahleel think?

"I want us to be together."

Jahleel had sweetly told her multiple times that he wanted them to be together. That the long distance shouldn't be a factor, that God would work out the details. If Bebe got this job, that was a very necessary detail. Despite not making any declarations of love, she knew she loved Jay. It was just too scary to admit, even to herself. But he deserved her courage. After all, he'd shown her daily that he would always show up. He wasn't like Will by a long shot.

Still, she'd need to find some way to see how Jahleel felt about her going to Texas. And she needed to make a decision about Will wanting to sever his parental rights. Her divorce decree said she couldn't take Hope out of the state without Will's permission. But if she signed that paper, her movements would be a nonfactor. Still, if she told Hope, would that ruin the holidays for her little one?

Lord, so much to think about. So much I want to hide from.

"At least I tried." May's words repeated in her mind. Did Bebe want to live life wondering *what if*? What if she didn't follow Jay to Texas?

She dialed her principal.

"Bebe, you miss school already?"

She let out a shaky laugh. "I have a hypothetical question for you."

"O-kay." Andrea drew out. "Shoot."

"If I were to quit, would you be able to find a replacement in time for the New Year?"

There was a pause. "Interesting you should ask."

"Oh?" She sank onto a barstool. "Why?"

"There's a local teacher interested in teaching kindergarten. Obviously, all positions are filled. This teacher is willing to leave their current position and move to another district but wishes to stay at Peachwood."

Is this Your doing, Lord?

"Are you thinking of leaving?" Andrea asked. "I know how to keep a confidence."

"I am," Bebe blurted. "I have an interview Monday."

"This wouldn't have anything to do with a certain football player?"

Bebe grinned. "Is nothing sacred?"

"You know how small Peachwood Bay is." Andrea laughed.

"I do," she sighed. She and Jay had been getting looks wherever they went. Some because he was Jahleel Walker, the famous football player, and others from former classmates who had watched them date in high school.

"Well, rest assured, if you wish to leave, we'd have no problem filling the spot."

"Thanks, Andrea."

"Good luck." Andrea hung up.

"What's an interview?" Hope asked.

Bebe gasped, placing a hand on her heart. "Where did you come from, pumpkin?" She scooped Hope into her arms and tickled her belly.

"Stop it," Hope giggled.

Bebe placed a kiss on her daughter's cheek and sat her back down.

"You didn't answer my question." Hope placed her hands on her hips.

Bebe held in a chuckle. "I'm sorry, I didn't realize you were my mother." She winked at Hope.

"Mama," she whined.

"An interview is when someone asks you questions to see if you would be good at a job or not."

"You already have a job."

Bebe bit her lip. Should she tell her? "Come sit next to me."

"Is something wrong, Mama?" Hope asked as she obeyed.

"No, pumpkin. I wanted to ask you a question."

"What?" Curiosity filled the green eyes just like hers.

"What would you think if we moved to Texas?"

Hope's eyes grew wide. "Texas? Why? Who do we know that lives there?"

"Jahleel lives there."

"No, he doesn't." Her nose wrinkled. "He lives with Reverend Walker."

"Actually, he doesn't. Since he hurt his leg, he's been staying with them so he can get better. But his home is in Texas."

"Would we live with him?"

Bebe's brain stalled. They weren't married, so of course not. But she'd be lying if she didn't admit that was her wish. But how did you explain all of that to a seven-year-old? *Help me, Lord.*

"We'd probably get our own place."

"But I thought you were going to marry him."

Bebe bit her lip. "Jay has never asked me, but I would love for him to." She blinked. The words seemed to blossom with hope inside of her. She would be happy to call herself Mrs. Jahleel Walker. She loved him so much. Bebe rushed on. "I like him. One day I would like to marry him. But right now, we're just dating. If we move to Texas, we would get to see him a lot more, and maybe one day that will happen."

"Would he come to all of my football games?"

"I'm sure he would." She hoped. Prayed. Wished. "But don't say anything to him. I need to have a grown-up conversation with him. Okay?"

"All right. Will Grandma and Grandpa know where to find us to come visit?"

Bebe nodded.

"Okay." Hope hopped off the couch. "Can I have the hot chocolate now?"

Bebe stared at her. *That was it?* No more questions? Hope looked at her expectantly. "I'll go make it right now."

"Thanks, Mama."

Jay knocked on Bebe's door. In no time, it swung open and Hope grinned up at him.

"Mama made hot chocolate, and she's making Christmas popcorn now."

"Christmas popcorn?" He closed the door behind him.

Bebe looked up from setting a bowl of popcorn on the coffee table. "Yep. It's got M&Ms, pretzels, sprinkles, and melted marshmallows."

"Wow, that sounds amazing."

She patted a couch cushion. "Come sit and elevate your leg."

He loved how she fussed over him. He sat down as she pressed play on the movie. Hope had a smaller bowl of popcorn and curled up in the recliner as she watched the movie from underneath a blanket.

"Happy the holiday break started?" he murmured to Bebe.

She sighed and leaned her head against him. "Blissfully happy."

"Good." He tucked an arm around her and pulled her close.

They said nothing as the movie started. Hope made comments from time to time—there hadn't been a movie they watched where she didn't commentate—but it was silent otherwise. Jay wanted to think that it was because they were all enjoying themselves, but he could feel stress coming from Bebe in waves.

What was bothering her? Before he could ask, the doorbell chimed.

Hope sat up. "Can I answer it, Mama?"

"That's fine."

Bebe turned to look at the door. Jahleel was glad they had a good view from here. He didn't really like the idea of Hope answering the door alone, but this was Peachwood Bay. Nothing bad happened here.

"Grandma!" Hope squealed.

"What?" Bebe stared in shock as her parents entered the house. "I thought you weren't coming until next week!"

"Surprise!" Mrs. Willabee said.

Bebe stood and hugged her mom, then her dad. "I can't believe y'all are here. I've missed you."

"How you doing, son?" Mr. Willabee asked Jay.

He stood and shook the older man's hand. "Getting better each day."

"Glad to hear it. Glad to hear it. Will you be back on the field?" he asked quietly.

Jay shook his head. "No."

"Sorry to hear that."

"It's okay, sir. I've got a bright future ahead."

Mr. Willabee looked behind him at Hope and Bebe, then back to Jay. "That you do."

"Look at you, Jahleel Walker," Mrs. Willabee interrupted. She held out her hands. "Give me a hug, young man."

"It's good to see you, Mrs. Willabee."

"Yes, it's been a long time." She stepped back and looked him over. "I hope that knee is treating you right."

"It's getting better." He held up the cane. "And I have help."

"Good, good."

Bebe motioned to the couch. "Sit. We're watching *The Polar Express* and eating a snack. Join us?"

"That's what we came up here to do. We couldn't let another day pass now that Hope is on break."

"So you'll be here the whole time?" Bebe asked.

"Yes. Do you have everything finished with the ball?" Mrs. Willabee asked.

Bebe looked at Jay. "We crossed everything off the list, right?"

"Just about. Although May and Ryan might need help with decorating."

Mrs. Willabee rubbed her hands together. "That sounds perfect. Just point me in the right direction, and I'll be of use."

"Talk to my mom," Jay said. "I'm sure she knows where help is needed the most."

"Great idea." Bebe's mother tilted her head. "How is she doing? And your father?"

"They're great. They were dancing in the kitchen the other day."

Bebe arched a brow. He loved the silent communication of *are you okay?* He nodded, and she smiled.

"Bill, why don't we dance in the kitchen?" Mrs. Willabee demanded.

"It's a galley kitchen. There's no room for that."

Mrs. Willabee huffed. "Well, that's going to be my Christmas wish from you."

He laughed. "Keep wishing, honey."

Jay tried to smother his laugh, but a snort came out. Bebe's mother whipped her head around so fast he was shocked she didn't hurt her neck.

"Are you laughing, Jahleel Walker?"

"No, ma'am."

"Hmmph. You better not be."

163

Bebe winked at him.

Soon they all settled down to watch the movie once more. Occasionally Bebe's folks made eye contact with him, noting the lack of distance between him and Bebe, but they said nothing.

Unease coiled in his gut. Were they unhappy about their relationship? Did they wish Bebe hadn't given him a second chance? After talking with Ryan, Jahleel knew convincing Bebe he was a better man and here for the long haul was something that had to be done. But he'd never factored in how her folks would feel about their relationship. His mom was happy that he was dating Bebe. She'd always liked her and had no qualms. Then again, Bebe hadn't been the one to break his heart. He'd broken hers.

So have a conversation with her folks. Reassure them.

He could do that, he just didn't know when. It certainly wouldn't be while munching on Christmas popcorn and watching *The Polar Express.*

Once the movies were over, Jahleel stood up. "I'm gonna head home." He gave a side hug to Bebe as her parents looked on. "See you tomorrow?" he murmured.

"Yes, please," she whispered.

"Perfect." In a louder voice he spoke to her folks. "Goodnight, Mr. and Mrs. Willabee."

"Goodnight, Jahleel. Tell your mama I'll be over tomorrow, 'kay?" Bebe's mother smiled.

"Will do."

"How about I walk you out?" Mr. Willabee asked.

Jay nodded. Now they could talk about the elephant in the room instead of ignoring it. Jay kissed Bebe's cheek and headed toward the front door. Mr. Willabee motioned for Jay to go first. Once the door clicked closed behind them, Jay breathed out a sigh.

"There's something I need to say, sir."

"I'm sure there is, but let me go first." Mr. Willabee crossed his arms over his chest.

"Yes, sir."

"What you did to Bebe when y'all were in high school was foul. But you were young, so I gave you a pass."

This didn't sound good. "But . . ."

"But y'all aren't kids anymore. I need to know your intentions, or I will steer her clear of you in a heartbeat."

"Sir, I want forever with Bebe. I want to be a father to Hope if Bebe will let me. I'm not trying to mess with her heart or break her trust ever again."

Mr. Willabee studied him. "Does she know this?"

"Kind of."

"Explain."

"She knows I want to be with her and that I'll figure out the details as to when and where. I have loose ends in Texas I need to tie up."

"Then you're moving back here?"

"Not necessarily. We haven't really talked about that. I expect that will come once we've been together longer. I don't want to rush her."

"That makes sense."

"But I haven't told Bebe I want to be a father to Hope. She's still trying to figure out the whole situation with Will."

"Hold up." Mr. Willabee held up a hand. "What situation with Will?"

Shoot. Did he not know? "Sir, I don't want to break a confidence."

"I get that, but if I need to go find that knucklehead and knock him into next week, you need to let me know."

Jay shifted his feet. Did he owe Mr. Willabee the information? He'd been taught to respect his elders, but this was Bebe's business and only hers. If she wanted her folks to know, she would've told them, right? "Sir, I'd feel better if you talk with Bebe. I don't want to say anything."

The man looked him up and down, and then respect shone in his eyes. "Very well. I'll do that." He offered a hand.

Jahleel shook it. "Have a good night, sir."

"Don't hurt my baby girl, and we'll get along just fine."

"That's the last thing I want."

"Goodnight, Jahleel."

He took that as a sign of dismissal and made the way across the grass and onto his parents' front porch. It had been an interesting conversation, and the band around his chest loosened. It wasn't perfect parental approval, but it was a step in the right direction.

Chapter
SIXTEEN

She'd gotten the job.

Bebe stared in shock at the email in her inbox. All necessary onboard paperwork had been attached. When she'd had May press submit on the application, part of her had figured there was no way she would get the job. She lived in Georgia, for goodness' sake.

Yet God had aligned everything perfectly.

Only she hadn't talked to Jay about the possible move yet. She wanted to get his thoughts, but then her folks had come into town early. She'd spent time with them doing all the fun holiday things like night fishing, fudge making, and Christmas caroling at the assistant living facility a couple of blocks away.

Jay had come over to help them make fudge and had sung horribly off-key while caroling. And every time, they'd exchanged glances as if to say *I miss you, I wish we could be alone, this is the best Christmas ever.* But nothing aloud to each other.

Now that she had the offer letter and contract in hand, she had to tell Jay. But first, she needed to talk to her folks.

She closed her laptop and headed for the kitchen. If the

scents wafting from the kitchen were any indication, her mom was making homemade cider for them to enjoy later.

"Hey, sweetie, can you grab the cloves for me?"

"Sure." Bebe grabbed the spice container and handed it to her mom. "You making cider?"

"Yes. Hope said y'all haven't had any yet this season."

"Nope, just hot chocolate."

"That was always your favorite." Her mom smiled, studying Bebe. "Looks like something's on your mind." She placed the lid on the pot. "Want to talk about it?"

Bebe nodded. "Will wants to sever his parental rights."

"What on earth?" Her mom's jaw dropped. "Are you fooling around with me?"

"No, ma'am. Not about something like that."

"What are you going to do? Are you going to fight him on it? Or . . ."

Bebe drew in a deep breath. "I don't know. I've been praying and . . ." She swallowed. "Well, things between me and Jay are really good, Mama. I . . . I love him."

"Oh, sweetie." Her mama cupped her face. "Don't you remember what happened the last time you gave your heart to that boy?"

"Of course. It's one reason I was so hesitant to start something in the beginning. But he's not the same man, I'm not the same woman, and now . . . everything just feels right."

"Then what has you anxious? Is it just the stuff with Will?"

"I applied for a job in Texas and got it. It's mine if I want it, and it starts the day after New Year's."

Her mom sagged against the kitchen cabinet. "Bebe, I'm not sure how much shock I can take." She pointed to the barstools. "Let's sit."

They sat down, and Bebe swiveled the stool to face her mom. "If I sign the paperwork Will gave me, aren't I telling Hope that she's fatherless? And even though I've told her God is a father to the fatherless, I don't actually want her to be without one." Her tears welled up.

"I understand those feelings, sweetie, but you have to remember that Will is doing this, not you."

True, but . . . "Do you think I should sign, then?"

"First, let's talk about Jay. Are you sure about him?"

"Yes."

"One hundred percent?"

"Yes. He's been amazing, Mama. He watches holiday movies with me and Hope. He went shopping with me for the ball. He comes to Hope's football games. Not to mention the dates and sweet moments we've shared. It's like high school but so much better. We've been honest about our fears, and we both want a relationship that will last. Neither of us is shying away from commitment."

"Well, obviously, applying for a job in Texas shows your commitment, but what is he doing to show you his?"

"Besides showing up? Because you know that's something Will would've never done."

"I know, honey. I just . . ." Her mom sighed. "I don't want you following a man."

"I'm not. Jay hasn't asked me to make the move. If anything, he's been telling me to trust God for the details. Well, this job fits perfectly, and Andrea told me there's a local teacher who wants the kindergarten spot if I leave."

"If you're that committed, you're envisioning marriage, I assume."

Bebe nodded.

"Then why not sign those papers from Will and let Jay adopt Hope? If you'll marry, you can make the transition so he's her father in every way."

Her mom had a point. Though they'd talked about their relationship, Bebe hadn't talked a lot about Hope and Jay's role in her life. Not because she didn't want to know, but because she was trying to stay present in the moment and not control every detail. Jay was wonderful with Hope, and Hope liked and respected him.

Ugh, why was conversation so necessary in every part of life?

"I guess I should talk to him," she said.

"Does that scare you?"

"A little."

"Why?" Her mom watched her expectantly.

"Communication has never been my strong suit. I don't know how to share my heart without fearing the outcome."

"But you said Jay has shared with you and vice versa."

She nodded. "He has. He doesn't want to make the same mistakes."

"Then you don't either. Talk to him, Bebe. Go from there."

"You're right."

She could just head over to the Walker residence and bare her heart. Surely Jay wanted the same things she did, so this conversation was merely a formality. Nothing shocking had to be said.

Bebe grabbed a light jacket and headed outdoors. There was a cold front expected tonight, but so far the temperatures remained mild. She rapped her knuckles on the front door as her mind thought of talking points.

The door opened, and Jay smiled at her. "Hey, you. I wasn't expecting you."

"I know, but I wanted to see you." She bit her lip. "You busy?"

"Nah, just watching the game."

"Basketball?"

Jay nodded. "Do you want something to eat or drink?"

"No."

"Come here." He held out his arms.

Bebe walked straight into them, resting her head against his chest. She let out a sigh as her body melted against his. He wrapped his arms around the small of her back. She felt safe. There was nowhere else she'd rather be, but voicing that seemed so scary. She'd had so many conversations with Will where she'd been silenced or cut off.

She pulled back and looked up into Jay's eyes. "I'm glad you asked me to think about us, to consider giving us a second chance."

His lips curved up. "I'm glad you gave me one."

"If you were to dream about our future, what does it look like?"

"I like this game." He rubbed her back. "I see us married and having one or two more kids who resemble Hope and have your beautiful green eyes."

Her eyes watered. He wanted their kids to look like Hope? "Would you ever consider adopting her?"

"I would be honored." He pulled back some, still holding her at the elbows. "Are you going to sign Will's papers?"

She bit her lip. "I think so. He hasn't been a part of her life for so long, it kind of makes sense to do so. And if we're planning on forever . . ."

Jay kissed her forehead. "Yes. Sign the papers. I'd happily adopt her."

One thing off her mind. Now for the other. "In your future dreams of us, are we in Georgia?"

Jay slowly shook his head. "No."

"Would you want me to move to Texas?" She bit her lip.

"Only if you wanted to and were comfortable with it. Nothing says we have to live in Texas, but I also don't think Peachwood Bay is for me."

"Understood." She stepped out of his arms and made her way to the couch. "Then I have something to say."

Jahleel wanted to hide in his room and avoid whatever it was that Bebe had to say. Had she brought up his hopes and dreams just to dash them with an *it's not you, it's me* speech?

"What's up?" He angled himself so he could face her on the couch.

"I applied for a job in Texas, but then I realized maybe we needed to have a talk, and I—"

He cut her off. "Are you serious? Did you get it? Are you interested in moving there, or do you think this is something you *have* to do?" His words rushed out, but he couldn't stop them. He was torn between elation at her taking a step toward forever and worry that he'd somehow made a move to Texas seem like a must.

"You've never made it seem like I had to move to Texas." Bebe laid a palm over his hand. "I kept thinking about the probability of you moving here, and it just never seemed right. But there is nothing keeping me here other than a job."

"So you found a new one?"

"Yes. If I accept, I start after the New Year."

His mouth dropped open. "Bebe . . ."

"You're not the only one who doesn't want to part, Jahleel Walker."

Happiness shot through his heart. He leaned forward, cupping her face, and finally kissed her like he'd wanted to do for weeks. She let out a sigh as she wrapped her arms around his neck. Her lips were as familiar as yesterday and as new as future promises.

The sound of footsteps started in the hall. He scooted back and winked at her just as his father walked into the living room.

"Bebe, I didn't know you were here."

"Hi, Reverend Walker. I was just visiting Jahleel." She pointed to him as if his dad didn't recognize his own son.

Instead of scoffing or saying something rude, his dad cracked a smile. Jay almost fell over at the sight. Yep, God was working miracles left and right. Maybe his father's heart really had grown.

"It's been nice seeing you two around here," his father said.

"Your son is great." Bebe smiled softly at him.

"He is. I'm glad you see that too." His father waved awkwardly. "Well, I've got to work on my sermon for tomorrow."

"Praying all the words come together, Dad," Jay said.

Surprise filled his father's eyes. "Thank you."

As soon as he left, Bebe let out a small "Wow."

"Surprised we can be civil?" Jay asked.

"That was more than civil. That was kindness, and I think I saw him smile."

Jahleel laughed. "I had the same thought. We had a good talk the other day, and he's been trying."

"And you're good? Happy with the talk and the outcome?"

He nodded.

"I'm so glad, Jahleel."

"So am I. Who knew I needed to come back home?"

"God. You remember, He's in the details."

"Thank goodness. Every time I got in the mix, things went south real fast."

She chuckled. "Agreed. And that *wow* . . . it was also about that kiss."

He grinned. "We should do that more, but maybe when my dad's not in the house."

"Agreed."

"What should we do tonight?"

"Hmm, I don't know. I plan on waking up early tomorrow. Hope wants reindeer pancakes for her birthday."

"Reindeer pancakes?" He stared into Bebe's pretty green eyes. "You're an amazing mom, you know that right?"

"I just want her to feel special on her day. It's so hard having a birthday right before Christmas. I want her to know that even though we're celebrating Christ the next day, I'll never forget how I got my own special bundle the night before."

"I got her something."

Bebe looked at him in confusion. "What do you mean?"

"I got Hope a gift."

Her mouth parted, and tears welled in her eyes. "Are you serious, Jahleel Walker?"

"Of course. I had to. It's her birthday. It's not every day a girl turns eight."

Bebe sniffed. "Why are you so awesome?"

"Georgia-made, darlin'."

Her head fell back as laughter rang around the room. "Oh, goodness. I forgot you had an ego on you."

"Nah, it's fake bluster. If you see anything awesome in me, it's because you're too kind. I'm just me."

"Yeah, but you got my baby a birthday gift."

"And I can't wait to get you one on yours."

She rolled her eyes, but a smile lit her face. "That's far away. But I thank you for already thinking of me."

"Always." He tucked a strand of hair behind her ear. "I did get you a Christmas gift."

"When will I get it?" Anticipation lit her eyes.

"On Christmas, duh."

She chuckled. "Aren't you and your folks going to be spending quality time with each other?"

"Of course we will, but you live right next door. It's not a hardship to carve out time and exchange gifts."

"Good, because I can't wait for you to see yours."

They made plans for the ball and then for Christmas Day. For the first time in a long time, Jahleel couldn't wait to spend the holiday in Peachwood Bay. With conversation between him and his father going more smoothly and cementing his relationship with Bebe, Christmas had once again brought joy to his heart. He knew that the holiday wasn't about getting what he wanted, but the gifts of a better relationship with his dad and a restored one with Bebe felt like Christmas miracles.

God cared about Jahleel, even when his focus was elsewhere. Not that he hadn't been thinking about the Lord this season. After all, he'd begun starting his morning by listening to the Bible as he did his physical therapy. Once he was ruled healthy, he'd go back to running in the mornings and continuing to listen to the Bible via audiobook.

No, this Christmas he'd had his whole mindset reset. God had gotten Jahleel to see what was important: the relationships he'd been blessed with. If it weren't for his injury, he would've kept ignoring his parents and missed out on getting to know Bebe again and falling in love with her.

Thank You for allowing me to see what really matters. May I never take my family and friends for granted. Please bless my relationship with Bebe and Hope. Please continue to reconcile my relationship with my dad. In Jesus's name, amen.

Chapter
SEVENTEEN

Bebe did a small twirl before stopping in front of her full-length mirror. The emerald-green dress was perfect for the Christmas party. The tulle bottom added a whimsical touch. It wasn't something she'd normally pick out, but Hope wanted to match. The color added depth to the green of their eyes, and the twirling action of the skirt was plain fun. Anticipation rolled in her stomach. She couldn't wait for tonight as they celebrated the reason for the season. She added red dangling earrings and red bangled bracelets to her right hand to complete the look.

"Hope," she called out. "You ready?"

Since Jahleel had offered to pick up Bebe and Hope, her parents had already left for the ball. They hadn't wanted to infringe upon *the young couple*, as her dad referred to them. They'd offered to bring Hope with them, but Bebe wanted to be near the birthday girl.

Her daughter came running into the room and stopped, covering her mouth. "You look like a princess, Mama."

"No way. I'm pretty sure you're the princess tonight." She

held out her arms, bending down to wrap her Christmas blessing in a hug. "Happy birthday, pumpkin."

"You already said that, silly."

"You know I can't help myself."

Hope smiled and kissed her cheek. "Let's go. I want to dance." She twirled around in her matching dress, giggling as the skirt billowed out.

Bebe grabbed their coats and headed for the front door. After putting them on, she opened the door and stopped. Santa was outside talking to Jahleel.

"Santa!" Hope shrieked. She looked in shock at the sleigh. "Reindeer! This is the best birthday ever!" She tugged on Bebe's hand.

Bebe stared down at her pride and joy. "You like?"

"I love! He even looks real," Hope whispered, pointing to Mr. Hammond.

"I thought so too."

Hope skipped toward the sleigh. Santa wasn't something they celebrated at home, but Hope loved the idea of him regardless. Her girl would probably squeal all the way to the town hall.

Jay helped Hope up into the sleigh, then turned toward Bebe. He looked breathtakingly handsome in his tuxedo. His broad shoulders seemed to be emphasized in the black jacket, and the cane at his side only made him look more dashing.

He made a circular motion with his finger. Bebe grinned and did a slow three-sixty.

"You look beautiful, Bebe."

"So do you."

He blushed. "Let me help you into the sleigh."

"Thank you, but I thought the sleigh rides were starting at the church? Isn't that what was discussed?"

"Originally, but since there was time between when service

ended and when the ball starts, Mr. Hammond suggested we just stop at routes around the town to carry folks to town hall. His son started across town first."

"Oh my goodness, this is great. Thank you."

"Yes, thank you, Mr. Walker," Hope gushed. "This is the best ever!"

Jay tapped her nose. "I have a special gift for you later."

"For me?" Her eyes widened.

"Of course. Someone told me you were an old lady today. Eight years old."

She giggled, eyes bright. "I'm younger than you."

"We won't talk about how young I am." He gently nudged Hope. "I had to get my favorite player a gift for her birthday."

Hope's cheeks bloomed with excitement as Jay continued to tease her.

When they walked into the town hall, Bebe gasped. Snowflake angels hung from the ceiling in between red and green streamers. Each angel was different. Some with big wings, some with little ones, and others without. And they were all different colors. Not to mention there were three different Christmas trees displayed throughout the room. One all red, another all white, and the last pure gold.

"It's so pretty," Hope said in a hushed whisper.

Bebe nodded. "It is. May and the others did a great job."

"Of course I did."

Bebe whirled around to see May in a red dress. The chiffon material clung to her lithe frame. "You look gorgeous." She hugged her friend. "And the place looks phenomenal."

"We had fun making the angels." May sent a smile Ryan's way.

"I'll bet. I've barely talked to you this week." Bebe wanted to be sad, but she understood. Both of them had found love this Christmas. However, Bebe knew she and May would continue to be the best of friends.

"Likewise." May winked and then turned to Hope. "Happy birthday!"

"Thank you, Ms. May!" Hope turned to Bebe. "Mama, can I go find my friends?"

"Sure."

Hope walked away, doing a few twirls here and there.

Jahleel cleared his throat. "I'm going to go talk to Ryan. Save me a dance?"

"Of course."

"Then I'll be right back." He kissed her forehead and walked away.

"Wow, y'all two are adorable." May grinned.

Bebe waited until Jahleel was out of earshot. "Doesn't he look perfect in that tux?" she sighed.

"Not as handsome as Ryan." May hooked her arm through Bebe's. "I'm going to miss you, friend."

"Me too." She bumped May's hip. "You better visit."

"Maybe after the honeymoon." May smirked.

"Ha ha." May would probably take a long time before she said *I do* to Ryan. Not because she was gun-shy like Bebe had been, but because May did most things slow and steady. It was one reason her decision to move to Nashville seemed so out of the blue. Only May hadn't been able to find a job up there yet and refused to move until she did.

"Since you haven't found a job yet, what will you and Ryan do?"

"We'll visit every other weekend until the school year's over. I'm hoping by then I'll have a new job."

"I'm so proud of you, May. I know I was really hesitant about your relationship at first, but you're going after what you want. I admire that."

May leaned her head against Bebe's. "Thanks, girl. I'm proud of you too."

Bebe was proud of herself. Once she laid her fears down

before God, He'd given her the courage to move forward. He'd also provided her with wise counsel so she could see the areas she fell short and needed help to move forward.

"I'm so thankful for your friendship, May. You've been a huge blessing in my life."

"Likewise. And remember, live. Don't let Will take your joy."

"I won't." She looked at her friend. "I signed the papers."

"How do you feel about that?"

"It hurt, but I trust God. He has great things in store for Hope. Me trying to make Will be a father just because we had a child was only preventing me from healing and hurting Hope with the constant expectation. Now, maybe she can heal."

"And maybe a new, better father is in her future." May did a head nod toward Jahleel.

Bebe's cheeks heated when she saw Ryan and Jahleel looking at them. "Are they talking about us?"

"Or inviting us to dance."

They walked toward the men.

"May I have this dance?" Jahleel asked.

Bebe nodded.

Jahleel guided her to the dance floor, then slid his arms around Bebe's waist. She rested a hand on his chest. "You look so dreamy in this tuxedo."

"I've got nothing on you, baby. Green is definitely your color."

He twirled her away, then brought her flush against him. Her body warmed from the move. "Where did you learn to do that?"

"Believe it or not, watching my parents."

"Wow."

"Shocking, right?" He chuckled.

"A bit. I don't know what's more shocking, you being able to do it after merely watching, or them dancing."

"They took dance classes."

Her mouth dropped open.

Jahleel threw his head back and laughed. "You look just like I did." He nuzzled his nose into her hair. "Bebe Willabee, I love you."

Her heart stopped, then started double-time. "I love you too, Jahleel." A sigh of contentment left her lips.

"You do?"

"Completely."

Jahleel kissed the edge of her jaw, slowly moving upward. When their lips brushed, Bebe sighed. He pressed his mouth firmly against hers, then drew back. "Don't want my father upset if we go past a PG rating."

She chuckled. "This has been the best Christmas ever."

"It really has."

Jahleel loved the feel of Bebe in his arms. He was so thankful that she loved him as much as he loved her, enough that she'd willingly move to San Antonio.

Since their talk, he'd been looking at storefronts to set up his shop. He might have found the perfect location, but it was something he wanted to talk to her about. If they were going to start a life together in Texas, he wanted to make sure Bebe was there with him every step of the way.

He'd already looked into a moving firm to get her stuff into San Antonio and called a realtor to find her a temporary place to stay. Because if he had anything to say about it, they would be married and living in his place sooner rather than later.

The music came to a stop, and they turned. His father stood on the stage with a microphone. His sermon earlier that day had many of the congregants reaching for a tissue to wipe the tears from their eyes. Jay wasn't sure what his mother had started in his father, but he could honestly say that was the best preaching his father had ever done.

"Merry Christmas, Saints!" the Reverend boomed.

"Merry Christmas," they chorused.

"I'd like to give thanks to some people." He began listing all the people involved in putting the ball together. People cheered at each name. "Last, I'd like to thank my son. He kindly footed the bill so that any donation on your part would go to the recipients of the angel tree."

Jahleel flushed. He'd had no idea his father would openly admit such a thing. Jahleel dipped his head in gratitude.

"You all ensured that every person on the tree received a Christmas gift this year. We have it on good authority that the presents have been delivered, and there will be many smiling faces tomorrow morning."

The crowd cheered louder than ever.

"We also collected an extra two thousand dollars from the offering at today's service, which will go to the local food pantry."

Cheers and applause filled the room.

"May God remember your kindness to those in need. Let's keep the spirit of giving alive and well throughout the rest of the year." His father paused. "Now, let's have fun."

His father met Jahleel's gaze and gave a simple nod. The work in their relationship was slow going, but Jay had seen it progress, and that was enough for him. Knowing he could return to Peachwood Bay and be welcomed by both of his parents had gone miles in healing hurt from the past. And knowing that his parents planned to visit him in the future was proof that his dad was working to bridge the gap between them.

Hope ran up to them. "I want to dance too."

"Then let's do this," Jay said. He took Hope's hand, and Bebe took the other, and they danced around in a circle as if it was always meant to be that way.

When it came time for the ball to end, Jahleel drove Bebe and Hope back home. Before the women got out of the car, he pulled an envelope from his inside coat pocket. He turned to look in the backseat.

"Ms. Hope, this is for you."

She frowned at the envelope. "What's this?"

"Your birthday gift."

Interest piqued, she opened it and pulled out three tickets. "Tickets? What for?" She squinted, then screamed in delight.

He winced at the high-pitched sound.

"Hope Gordon!" Bebe scolded.

"Sorry, Mama, but he got me three tickets to the Super Bowl!"

Bebe gawked at him.

"Hope that's okay?" he murmured.

"Are you serious? That's amazing."

He let out a breath.

"Thank you so much, Mr. Walker!" Hope threw her arms around him.

"Do you think you can call me Jay?"

She looked at Bebe, who gave a small nod. "Thanks, Jay."

"My pleasure. I hope you'll let me come with you."

Her grin grew wider. "Definitely. Mama too."

"I wouldn't miss it for the world," Bebe said.

"Wait until I tell my friends." Hope threw her arms in the air. "Best birthday ever!"

EPILOGUE

Jahleel looked around Bebe's home on Christmas Day. Her parents sat on the sofa, whispering to each other. Hope sat on the floor, happy with her new dolls. And his folks had actually come over to celebrate Christmas with Bebe and her folks as well. His father sat in the recliner while his mom was perched on his lap. Almost all of the presents had been distributed except the one burning a hole in his pocket.

He drew in a deep breath, then cleared his throat. "Um, excuse me. I think we forgot something."

Hope looked at him and winked. He hid a smile, trying not to give anything away. But Hope knew what was about to happen after they'd talked at the ball last night.

"What?" Mrs. Willabee asked.

"I have one more present." He looked at Bebe. "I almost forgot to give it to you."

"What are you talking about? The emerald necklace you gave me is perfect."

The 14k-gold halo pendant looked perfect around her neck, but that gift was just a warm-up. The one he really wanted to give came in a ring-sized box.

"What would you say if I told you that wasn't your real gift?"

She bit her lip. "Then this is fake?"

"Not at all. It's just that of all the jewelry you could possibly be wearing, a necklace isn't what I'd pick for you."

A cute blush warmed her cheeks. "Jay . . ." she whispered.

"Oh my goodness," his mom exclaimed.

Jahleel grabbed his cane, then lowered himself onto his good knee. "Bebe Willabee, walking away from you twelve years ago was the stupidest thing I've ever done."

Her eyes filled with tears.

"And when I came back here, I quickly wanted to make up for lost time." He reached for her hand. "I love you, Bebe, and I want nothing more than to spend the rest of my life with you." He paused, struggling with emotion. "Will you do me the honor of marrying me?"

"Oh, Jahleel." She sniffled as tears spilled down her cheeks. "Yes. Of course I'll marry you."

Of course. The words resonated in his head as his heart filled to the brim. He loved that it was a no-brainer *yes* for her, because he'd been a nervous wreck talking to Hope about it and asking Mr. Willabee for his blessing.

Seeing the joy on Bebe's face only increased the happiness he felt. His hands shook as he placed the ring on her finger. She wrapped her arms around his neck, and their lips met in a cumulation of their feelings. The kiss said *I love you, I can't wait to be your wife, you've made me so happy.*

Jay broke their kiss and smoothed her hair away from her face. "I love you," he murmured.

"And I love you."

He turned and motioned for Hope to join their circle.

"Do you like the ring, Mama?"

"I love it."

"I told Jay you would. He didn't believe me." Hope scoffed, then grinned.

Bebe looked confused. "You already knew?"

"Yep."

Jay chuckled. "Had to make sure she was okay with it."

"He asked for my blessing too," Mr. Willabee said.

His mom came over to the couch. "Let me see."

Soon his folks and her folks were congratulating them both and calling for a toast for a blessing on their marriage. Seeing both of their families together did something to Jay's heart. He never knew how much he'd needed to see this, but he was so thankful that being sidelined with an injury put him on the right route.

His days of football were over, but instead of feeling like the world had come to an end, he knew it was only just beginning.

AUTHOR'S NOTE

Dear Reader,

Thank you so much for reading *The Christmas Catch*. I hope it put you in the holiday mood. May you find someone to watch a Christmas movie with, drink hot chocolate with (don't forget the peppermint stick and marshmallows), and dance the night away with . . . even if it's in your kitchen.

When I wrote this story the first time, I wanted a touch of football in a holiday book. I love the sport, and putting a bit of that into a book was so much fun. This time around, I wanted to bring you more Christmas and more hope that things can always change for the better.

I did use a bit of creative license when it came to Jahleel and healing his knee. I wanted you to see how the change in career affected him, but I also wanted him to go out and enjoy the Christmas festivities. Other than that, the book is as real as a contemporary romance can be. Thank you for your grace and understanding.

I'm praying this holiday season blesses you and yours.

Blessings,
Toni

ACKNOWLEDGMENTS

There's something about seeing a book in print for the first time that gets an author in their feels. But this book you're reading wasn't a one-person production.

I'd like to thank my editor Jessica Sharpe for wanting another Christmas story from me. *The Christmas Catch* was formerly known as *A Sidelined Christmas.* After reading the older version, Jess was ready to give this story new life. Thank you for believing in me and my writing. Thank you also to the cover design team, the interior design team, and all the others who have contributed to making this book into reality.

Next, Rachel McMillan, agent extraordinaire! You're amazing. Thank you for going to bat for me. For believing in my writing and encouraging me when I need it. I'm so glad to have you in my corner.

I'd also like to thank all my readers. Without you, I'd have no writing career. I thank you for preordering, for sharing about the cover, for telling friends and family about the book. However you spread the word, please know it means the world to me. Knowing you'll be reading this book makes all the tears and hard work so very worth it.

To my husband, for keeping me on track when I want to be lazy and read a book. Thanks for reminding me of how close I get to the finish line to make my deadline. Also, thanks for answering all my questions about football when my brain decided to vacate the premises. I love you!

To my boys, here's another romance book. One day I pray you meet a God-fearing woman who likes my writing and forces you to read my books. Then maybe you'll discover this acknowledgment and know how much I love you. If I can add an *I told you so* for just cause purposes, then here it is. Love you guys!

FOR MORE FROM TONI SHILOH,
read on for an excerpt from

You Make It Feel like Christmas

Starr Lewis returns home for the holidays, jobless and single, to attend her sister's wedding to Starr's ex-boyfriend. But when her brother's best friend offers to go with her to the wedding activities and she gives his struggling Christmas shop a makeover, she wonders if the holidays could bring her a love to keep all year long.

Available now wherever books are sold.

Chapter
ONE

Starr Lewis hated to return home a failure, but at least she had the cover of the holiday season to hide her embarrassment.

The wind whipped through her as she stepped off the train. She shuddered and drew her coat closed at the neck, then followed her fellow passengers up the escalator to the main building. The man in front of her held the door open, and she trailed in behind him. Warmth caressed her face in a greeting, chasing the chill away.

She sighed and took a moment to admire the arched ceiling over Union Station. People hurried around her as she made her way toward the front doors. Her brother Gabe was picking her up, which meant she'd have thirty minutes to kill until he showed up. Gabe was always late. *Always.*

Starr tightened her grip on the handle of her fuchsia carry-on and headed for Jamba Juice. A mix of passion fruit, mango, and strawberry would be just the thing to freeze out the hot shame of returning home jobless.

Who cared if she'd had a smoothie before leaving New York

City? One could never have too many. Besides, she needed the liquid goodness to chase away reminders of being laid off and forced to live in her childhood bedroom for who knew how long. Out of the five Lewis children, Starr was the only one who no longer held an illustrious career.

Shake it off. You're not a failure. This is just a setback.

Of epic proportions. Not only did she have to move back home, but her demise lined up perfectly with her sister Angel's Christmas Eve wedding. To Starr's ex-boyfriend. *Ugh. God, please help me. I'm not sure how I'll make it through the wedding without wanting to gag.*

The hits just kept on coming. She'd better order a large smoothie.

Kelly Clarkson's rendition of "I'll Be Home for Christmas" crooned through the speakers. Starr shook her head at the unnecessary reminder and slowed as she got in line at Jamba Juice. Her cell buzzed in her coat pocket. She moved off to the side, pulling out the pink-encased iPhone and checking the caller ID. "Where are you?"

"Calm down. I'm on Union Station Drive with all the taxis and tourists. Should I park around back, or can you come out front?"

Her bottom lip poked out as dreams of smoothie bliss evaporated. "I'll be out front in a sec."

"Don't sound so enthused."

"I'm just a little hungry."

"You mean hangry? Well, grab some food then. But keep in mind I'm taking up space, and security might be giving me the side-eye—"

"All right, I get it," she snapped. The moment Gabe had said he was at the front entrance, she'd started walking that way.

Starr exited through the double doors and searched the cars lined up in front of her. "Are you in your car?"

"Dad's. My car died last week."

She sighed in relief when she spotted the familiar black Mercedes. "I see you." She headed his way, dragging her carry-on behind her.

"I see you too." Gabe popped out of the driver's door and came around the passenger side as he pocketed his phone. "Sis!" He picked her up, twirling her around.

She chuckled at his exuberance. "Put me down." Her head spun, but she soon caught her bearings. As she peered into Gabe's familiar features a pang twinged in her chest. Gabe was probably her favorite sibling. Her older brother also had the smoothest skin she'd ever seen. Probably beat out women who held a daily regimen of wrinkle-free cream and exfoliation. He definitely fit into the pretty-boy category.

"Did you miss me?" He waggled his eyebrows, then grabbed her suitcase.

"Maybe." Her lips twitched.

"Yeah, you did." He winked at her and closed the trunk. "Don't stand there all day. Mom and Dad are holding Thanksgiving dinner just for you."

Thank goodness. She was starved. She slid onto the passenger seat and buckled her seat belt. "That explains why I didn't have to wait too long."

"Ha." He shrugged. "What can I say? Life is meant to be enjoyed, not hurried."

"No one says you have to rush for everything. Just be on time for what's important."

"Like picking up my little sister?" He tossed an amused expression her way before turning to look at the road.

"Exactly." She slid her frozen hands under her thighs. "It's so cold here. It wasn't even this cold in New York."

"Oh, look at me," Gabe said in a high-pitched voice. "I just came from New York, and like"—he flipped his imaginary long hair— "I'm such a cosmopolitan now. DC is beneath me and all that I know."

She smacked his arm. "I'm just making a weather observation."

"For now."

Same ol' Gabe. She rolled her eyes. "How's everyone?"

"The same. Noel is going to work himself into an early grave. Eve is following in his footsteps, and Angel is Angel." He shrugged as he navigated through DC traffic.

Wreaths hung about the city streetlights as they had every Christmas since Starr could remember. She couldn't help the smile that tilted her lips. "It's good everything's the same."

"Is it?"

"Sure." Well, maybe the physical things. She didn't want to walk in the house and have everyone treat her like the baby just because she was the youngest Lewis sibling. She wanted to be taken seriously, but losing her job wouldn't add points in that direction.

"I'm surprised your boss gave you such a long break. Mom said you don't have to go back until the day after New Year's. Is that right?"

"Yep. Nice, huh?" Though it wasn't a vacation but her being handed a severance package and two letters of recommendation.

But that tidbit was her secret.

Starr had packed her household goods into a storage unit before leaving the city and returning to DC. If she was smart with her money, she could pay for the unit for four months. Obviously, she'd have to come clean to her parents well before then. If she was still here in the springtime, there was no way her folks would believe she'd been given that long of a vacation. Then again, maybe telling them she was working remotely would help her save face.

That's lying.

She tensed. Hopefully by the end of the month, she'd find another job, and they'd be none the wiser.

"Suspiciously nice."

Starr looked at Gabe, hoping she was projecting a calm demeanor that belied the fast beating of her heart. "The company values their employees."

Only she hadn't been one of them. Layoffs had to happen, and someone had to go. Why not the hardworking PR associate who saved more butts than the others? She'd only worked for the company for two years, which meant she was the easiest to say good-bye to.

Story of her life.

Her ex, Ashton, had had no trouble saying good-bye after taking one long look at Angel.

"I see." Gabe met her gaze, raising an eyebrow in skepticism. "You know you can talk to your big brother, right? Tell me your worries. Your *secrets.*"

"I don't have any." She faced straight ahead, looking out the windshield, then gasped and leaned forward. "Is it snowing?"

"Just a few flakes. They didn't even salt the roads, so it's nothing."

"Or we'll get a bigger snowfall than expected and be trapped at home." She did *not* want to be trapped at home with all her siblings to poke their noses in her business.

"Works for me. I don't want to go to work tomorrow anyway."

Starr snorted. "Working for your parents is *so* difficult."

"Don't be jealous. You know Dad would give you a job if you wanted."

"I do *not* want to work in finance." She hated math. Had *always* hated math and had the grades to reflect that. Too bad everyone else in the family was a math genius.

Even Angel.

Lord, I pray that I hold up seeing Angel again. After all, she didn't intentionally steal my boyfriend. She's just . . . Angel.

A selfish, manipulative—

No, no. She really didn't think Angel was aware of how Starr truly felt. After all, Starr hadn't called her names or threatened bodily harm. After introducing her boyfriend to her sister, Starr had later listened incredulously as Angel described her meeting with Ashton as fate in some star-crossed-lover-type drama. Apparently, Ashton felt the same way. He dumped Starr so he could ask Angel out and live happily ever after.

Starr sighed.

"What's going on in that head of yours?"

"I was just wondering what the holidays will be like." She offered a stiff smile. "You know how Mom is."

Gabe grimaced. "Unfortunately. My prediction is full-on Christmas drama with an extra helping of wedding chaos thrown in."

Just what she feared. "Great."

"Hey, you wanted to come back. You didn't seem to mind missing the last couple of Christmases." Gabe glanced at her. "Why break the streak now?"

"Angel's getting married." As much as she had hurt Starr, Angel was still her sister.

"True, but you could've come down the day before and left after Christmas Day. No need to torture yourself the whole holiday season."

Except now Starr had nowhere else to go. Her severance package wouldn't have lasted long in New York. Staying with her parents would give her time to plan her next steps. Only, she couldn't let anyone know that.

She pushed aside her feelings and pasted on a smile. "I missed you guys."

Gabe snorted. "You mean your friends."

"What?" She gasped. "I love all of you guys."

"You never hung around us growing up."

"Well, it's not my fault Noel and Eve were so much older.

They've always had their own friends." Sometimes being born last was the pits. Starr had been lonely until she took matters into her own hands.

"True. But you didn't hang with me and Angel either."

"That's because you had your twin superpowers activated and didn't let anyone else in the club."

Gabe took advantage of the red light to give Starr a long look, confusion written all over his face. "Is that really how you felt?"

"It's the truth."

"Starr . . ." He sighed and hit the gas. The car lurched forward. "We never meant to exclude you."

"I get it. I'm the fifth and last kid. Everyone had already paired off by the time I could talk and play. I had to make my own friends in order to have some, not because I didn't love my family."

"I'm sorry, Starr."

She shrugged and looked out the passenger window. The Lewis family liked to portray themselves as close-knit, but she'd always been on the outside looking in. She didn't expect the holidays to change that. And Angel's wedding definitely wouldn't.

Maybe she'd be able to reconnect with some of her friends who still lived in the area. Anything to occupy her days and keep the melancholy at bay.

"I'll make it up to you, 'kay?"

"How?" She peeked at Gabe.

"You can hang out with me and my friends."

"Really, Gabe? I'm a little too old for the 'kid sister tagging along with the older brother' bit."

"You'll like them."

We'll see. "I'm sure."

He grinned, his straight teeth a testament to the years he'd worn braces. "Then it's settled."

"First, let's get through dinner."

Gabe turned down their street, and Starr's pulse picked up speed. The neighbors always joined forces to decorate for the Christmas season. She knew this week had been spent decorating the exteriors of the multimillion-dollar homes. Every house glowed with white lights. Starr sank into her seat as their whitewashed brick home came into view. Navy shutters surrounded the candlelit windows, and a silver wreath decorated the matching front door.

"The inside is decked out, isn't it?"

"From top to bottom. Mom decorated all yesterday."

Starr chuckled. Their mom was a little too enthusiastic about Christmas. It's why they all had Christmas names, even though Gabe and Angel were the only ones born in December. Every year, the day before Thanksgiving, her mom would pull out the decorations and play her Christmas music for "atmospheric purposes."

Gabe pulled into the garage, and Starr was out of the car before the garage door could close again.

"I'll grab your bag."

"Thanks, Gabe."

"Mom's probably in the kitchen."

Starr entered the house and headed straight to the kitchen. Her jaw dropped. Gone were the black cabinets and red backsplash. The room seemed bigger with white cabinetry and black fixtures. The sapphire-blue backsplash went with the silver and blue Christmas decorations her mother was fond of.

"Baby girl!" Her mom threw open her arms as she came around the island and swept Starr into a hug. "Happy Thanksgiving."

"Happy Thanksgiving, Mom."

"I'm so glad you're home. Now all my babies are home." She grinned at Starr and folded Gabe into a group hug.

After a few seconds, she stepped back.

"Gabe said dinner was on hold. I didn't mean to make you guys wait," Starr said.

"Gabe." Her mother's black brows dipped in consternation. "Dinner won't be ready for another thirty minutes." She shook her head. "He's just making trouble."

"Me?" He pointed to his chest in mock horror. "I'm the angel, unlike your middle-born daughter."

"Ha. Go take your sister's suitcase to her room."

"Yes, ma'am." Gabe strolled out of the kitchen with a parting wink to Starr.

"You changed it." Starr gestured around the kitchen. "It looks good, by the way."

"Thank you. Angel brought my ideas to life."

Of course Angel redesigned it.

"But don't worry," her mom continued, "your room is the same as you left it."

Starr paused, her hand in midair with the meatball she'd swiped from the appetizer tray. "You mean, *exactly* the same?"

"Of course. The cleaning staff go in to dust once a month and don't touch anything else."

"But I haven't lived here since college." She'd graduated five years ago and moved to New York shortly after. This was really the first time she'd been back home apart from a visit here and there while staying at hotels—because she could afford to.

"You'll always have a room here, baby. You know that." Her mom dipped her head and shook it at the same time.

Now would be a good time to inform Mom about her unemployed state, but that news could wait. Maybe after the wedding, when everyone returned to their regular schedules. "Is everyone coming to dinner?"

"Of course. Noel will be here straight from work. He said he invited a friend."

"A *girl*friend?"

Her mother rolled her eyes. "I wish. He's in his thirties, for goodness' sake. How much longer is he going to make me wait for grandchildren?"

"He's married to his work."

"Don't I know it. But ledgers don't produce living, breathing babies." Her mother turned a burner off as she checked on another pot. "Eve is already here. Her condo got flooded from an upstairs neighbor, so she's staying in her old room until the repairs are done."

"That's awful." *Guess I'm not the only one dealing with stuff.*

"It was just *terrible*. She lost everything."

Poor Eve. Starr straightened, then put on her calm façade. "And Angel?"

"Angel and Ashton will be joining us too."

Her stomach dropped. "He—they will?"

"Of course." Her mom gave her an odd look. "Wedding preparations are in full swing, and those two are never out of each other's sight."

Disgusting. What had she subjected herself to? Maybe she should've looked harder for a job in the city. Anything to avoid seeing her ex and sister fall all over each other.

Her mother stilled, her brow furrowing. "You aren't jealous . . . are you?"

"Of course not." Starr put her practiced *as if* expression on. She'd perfected the look in the Amtrak bathroom because she knew someone would ask at some point. "We're old history."

"Well, not that old. It was only two years ago you two were together."

Way to rub the salt in, Mom. "We weren't serious." Well, *he* hadn't been. She hadn't known how serious she'd been until he'd willingly parted ways to go after Angel.

"I didn't think so. You never introduced us to him."

"We lived in different states!" She stared at her mom, shock running through her.

"Oh, sweetie, that won't matter when you meet the right guy. You'll see."

If her mom was going to ignore how Angel and Ashton got together, Starr wouldn't be expecting any sympathy this holiday season. *Welcome home, Starr.* "I think I'll go up to my room."

"Be sure to change into something presentable."

Because her slacks and silk blouse were abhorrent? "Yes, Mother."

"Don't you 'Mother' me. We'll have company. Dress your best."

Of course. That was her mother's motto.

Chapter
ONE

*L*aissez les bons temps rouler!
  Somehow Tuck and I had driven right into the beginning of Mardi Gras season. We'd been in the car for more than ten hours since leaving Eastbrook and making our way to the Risen Star Stakes held at Fair Grounds Race Course in New Orleans. We planned on attending the race to check out Dream's competition.

I couldn't quite express what it felt like seeing purple, green, and yellow beads hanging from the branches of the trees. Surely that was just something from the movies, right? Had parade participants thrown them up there on purpose, or was it a bead toss gone wrong?

"Can you believe this?" I asked.

"The sights or something else?"

"That we made it on the Derby trail."

Dream had done well in the early prep races, and now he'd be participating in the championship series, consisting of sixteen races that would lead to twenty horses on the field of Churchill Downs to run the Kentucky Derby.

"You mean when you asked me to train Dream, you didn't actually think you'd make it on the Derby trail?" Tuck smiled at me from the driver's seat.

My breath hitched at those perfectly curved lips and baby-blue eyes. Why did my best friend always have to make me feel like I was in need of a fainting couch?

I swallowed. *Focus on his words.* "I'd hoped. But now that we're here . . ." I shook my head. "Seriously, Tuck, how did we get here?"

Risen Star was the first race on the Derby trail, but we'd chosen to instead participate in the Battaglia Stakes at Turfway Park in two weeks. Each race awarded a certain number of points for the first through fifth winners. The twenty horses with the most points were eligible for the Derby.

"Hard work."

His hard work. Sure, I'd picked the horse, but I hadn't been the one spending hours and days and weeks training the colt. Tuck had. Though I did give my opinion here and there.

"I can't begin to thank you enough." My fingers itched to squeeze Tuck's hand like I'd done numerous times. But I needed to get my heart rate back to normal and push those affectionate feelings aside before I could touch him platonically.

"No thanks necessary, Pipsqueak."

Well, there went those loving feelings.

Since Tuck and I had started working together, our friendship had taken a strange path. We'd gone from sharing everything with each other to Tuck putting up an invisible brick wall between us. He treated me more formally, like he'd once treated my dad, his old boss. Yet every now and again, the wall lowered, and he'd choose to call me by my childhood nickname. I couldn't remember how often he called me Pipsqueak prior to training my Thoroughbred, but now I heard the unflattering nickname way too often.

More than once I'd considered confessing my feelings to Tuck, but the longer I remained mute, the longer it seemed taboo to me. Tuck would most likely reject me with all the love and kindness that existed in him, but that goodness wouldn't lessen the blow. No matter how he cushioned his words, telling me I would simply remain his best friend would shatter my heart.

Unfortunately, I wasn't sure his returning my affections would be the best thing either. We'd never been anything but Tucker and Piper, the two kids seen running across my folks' estate, playing hide-and-seek or, once we got older, racing our horses. We were always together, and people naturally assumed that meant we were like brother and sister.

Only there wasn't a single ounce of sisterly affection for Tucker Hale in me. I stuck my hand out the window and let the warmth from the sun soothe me. It had been a lot colder in Kentucky when we'd left my farm.

I'd bought the property last July, throwing my folks for a loop. I could still remember the shocked look on my mother's face when I enlightened her regarding my plans.

"Piper, honey, we didn't even get to look at the place. What if they upped the price because you're a McKinney? How could you make this step without our guidance?"

Dad had winked at me. *"Now, Jackie, we raised Piper to be smart. I'm sure she handled it beautifully."*

I sighed as the memory faded.

"You're thinking awfully loud over there. Thinking 'bout your folks?"

"Yeah," I murmured.

Tuck sighed. "They show their love the only way they know how."

Which begged the question, How did I need to be loved? Was it ungrateful for me to want them to let me stumble a bit? As soon as they'd learned of my plans, they'd tried to step in and help. They'd offered to find a jockey to race Dream and even tried to pay for my farm. I'd had to beg them to let me be independent and trust I could handle the responsibility.

"I might be smothered by the end of the season."

Tuck laughed. "Jackie McKinney is a fashion icon in the Derby world. Surely her picking out outfits isn't all that bad."

I just stared at him while he tried to dial down his laughter.

"Okay, the last outfit made you look like a Stepford wife."

"It's not me." I shuddered thinking of the pale pink tweed skirt suit Mama suggested I wear at our last race.

"Keep gently reminding her of that, and she'll eventually get it."

I rolled my eyes. Maybe I needed to have a conversation with Dad. He was great at playing mediator when I thought Mama's guidance a little overbearing. I tried so hard not to show her how upset her suggestions made me.

"Don't slouch. People will wonder why you can't walk with confidence."

"Don't wear those colors. They're not good with your complexion."

"Always use the manners we raised you with. We don't want others to complain."

She was so focused on what other people thought. And I got it. I was, too, but I saved myself a little breathing room. Of course, I couldn't be mad at her, because she adopted me. Wasn't it ungrateful to be mad at a parent who'd done more for you than your biological parents had?

My bio parents had dropped me off at an orphanage in Ọlọrọ Ilé—an island country in the Gulf of Guinea—and left me without a backward glance. Believe me, I know. I had that one childhood memory of their departure to torture me. Their retreating backs and my wails were all I could recall of them. On the other hand, my adoptive parents had continuously poured their love and monetary blessings on me. I'd never wanted for anything . . . except a little more autonomy.

As the parent of an only child, a little breathing room wasn't something Mama knew how to give. She loved fiercely and with a side of a little-overbearing presence. She'd been unable to have biological children, and Dad said after the two long years of waiting for my adoption to finalize and for me to actually arrive in the States, it was too much turmoil to go through again. So I became an only child to wealthy parents who were royalty in the Kentucky Derby scene. Their horses had sired past Derby winners, and they enjoyed selling the foals to the highest bidder in hopes that history would repeat itself.

"I don't know when, but I have no doubt your mom will learn how to parent an adult and give you some space." Tuck's voice broke my silence.

"I hope you're right." Because I didn't look forward to another ten years of feeling like a child past the age of eighteen.

Tuck slowed the truck to idle in front of our hotel.

I looked up at the white building with a black awning over the front entrance. "These buildings are gorgeous."

"And right downtown where you wanted to be."

"That's because I was thinking of my stomach." I grinned. "I've been dreaming about gumbo and beignets ever since I've known we were coming."

Tuck laughed. "Are we going to try to catch a Mardi Gras parade or two as well?"

I shrugged. I was there to scope out the competition, and I hadn't really made any plan other than that. Knowing Tuck, he'd taken care of that for the both of us.

"What's your plan?" I asked him.

"I'll share with you. Don't worry."

"Okay."

After we found the guest parking lot, skipping valet service, I followed Tuck up the hotel steps. He handed our baggage to a bellboy, and then we went inside to check in. My eyes took in the swanky details of the place, and I recalled the first time I traveled with my parents. They always stayed in five-star hotels for the best accommodations. I had to admit, the hotel snobbery bug caught me. Only now it was my money paying for my room as well as Tuck's.

"We going to eat right away?" I asked.

"Definitely. I don't want you getting hangry."

I loved that crooked grin on his face. What would he do if I let my wobbly knees tip myself right against him where lips could meet? I turned away, feeling heat in every pore on my face.

The memory of our first meeting came to the surface.

"You the new kid?"

I'd tilted my head back, the sun silhouetting a kid's frame. Someone sat down next to me, and a young boy's face came into focus, showing blond hair and blue eyes. The complete opposite to my black eyes and short black hair. His skin was pale where mine was dark.

"Yes," I said, English feeling foreign on my tongue.

He stuck out his hand. *"I'm Tuck. My dad's the horse trainer."*

"Piper." We shook hands, and something clicked right into place.

I hadn't realized it then, but Tucker Hale had stolen my heart before I even knew what love was. From that day forward, I followed him around Bolt Brook on a daily basis. Tuck taught me how to skip rocks at the water hole. He was right next to me when I rode my first horse. He was there to wipe my tears when I fell off and to cheer me on when I got back up.

I hooked a thumb over my shoulder. "I'm gonna go shower and change, then."

"Sure thing."

Good grief. Attending races together now proved to be a lot more difficult than when we worked for my parents. I thought removing my family from the equation would make work easier, but it had only added a weird tension.

After checking out my room, I grabbed a fresh set of clothes and toiletries from my suitcase. I wanted to look my best for Tuck just in case he ever decided to open his eyes and see that we could be more.

At least, I think that was what I wanted. My mind was so conflicted. The risk of losing him as a friend or being rejected because of my ethnicity was too much. Mentally, I knew Tuck had never given me reason to believe my race was an issue. But when you spent the majority of your life being the only Black person in nondiverse spaces, you couldn't help but believe people were just keeping their racial judgments quiet.

I didn't want to believe that's what Tuck did, and for the most part, I could assure myself he wasn't like that. But then a little voice would whisper in my ear, and doubt would ensue.

Most of the time, I could be myself around Tuck without race entering my mind. Fortunately, he seemed to accept all of me. After all, this was the same guy who watched rom-coms with me because I liked them, not because he would choose that genre.

So how could I risk the one friendship I could never bear to lose?

I couldn't.

Wouldn't.

Right?

I shook my head and turned on the shower. Surely those troubles would be waiting for me another time, another day. I wouldn't give them any more headspace . . . for now.

Toni Shiloh is a wife, a mom, and an award-winning Christian contemporary romance author. She writes to bring God glory and to learn more about His goodness. Her novel *In Search of a Prince* won the first ever Christy Amplify Award. *Grace Restored* was a 2019 Holt Medallion finalist, *Risking Love* was a 2020 Selah Award finalist, *The Truth About Fame* a 2021 Holt Medallion finalist, and *The Price of Dreams* a 2021 Maggie Award finalist. A member of American Christian Fiction Writers (ACFW), Toni loves connecting with readers and authors alike via social media. You can learn more about her writing at ToniShiloh.com.

Sign Up for Toni's Newsletter

Keep up to date with Toni's latest news on book releases and events by signing up for her email list at the link below.

ToniShiloh.com

FOLLOW TONI ON SOCIAL MEDIA

Toni Shiloh, Author   @ToniShiloh   @ToniShilohWrite

You May Also Like . . .

Starr Lewis returns home for the holidays, jobless and single, to attend her sister's wedding to Starr's ex-boyfriend. But when her brother's best friend offers to go with her to the wedding activities and she gives his struggling Christmas shop a makeover, she wonders if the holidays could bring her a love to keep all year long.

You Make It Feel like Christmas by Toni Shiloh

Mackenzie Graham's work crush, Jeremy Fletcher, has barely noticed her—until they compete for the same much-needed promotion. But winning has less to do with work performance and everything to do with showing the most Christmas spirit. As their yuletide duel progresses, it might be more than a job they risk losing.

All's Fair in Love and Christmas by Sarah Monzon

Hollywood hair stylist Nevaeh loves making those in the spotlight shine. But when a photo of her and Hollywood heartthrob Lamont goes viral for all the wrong reasons, they suddenly find themselves in a fake relationship to save their careers. In a world where nothing seems real, can Nevaeh be true to herself . . . and her heart?

The Love Script by Toni Shiloh
LOVE IN THE SPOTLIGHT

BETHANYHOUSE